THE
CRYSTAL
CODE

A. K. MITCHELL

Qubit Press Australia

Independent Publishing House
Innovative Independent Publishing that Inspires Discovery
Brisbane, Queensland, Australia

www.QubitPressBooks.com

Copyright © 2025 A.K. Mitchell
All rights reserved.
Published by Qubit Press Australia
Cover design & logo © 2025 Qubit Press Australia
National Library of Australia Cataloguing-in-Publication Data available.
ISBN: 9781764306218

Disclaimer

This is a work of fiction. Names, characters, organisations, places, events, and incidents are either products of the author's imagination or real place names used fictitiously. Any resemblance to actual persons, living or dead, or to actual events is purely coincidental. The scientific concepts, technologies, and theories described in this book are speculative and presented for narrative purposes only. They should not be interpreted as factual, predictive, or representative of real-world research or entities. The author and publisher make no representations or warranties with respect to the accuracy or completeness of the fictional material contained herein. Reader discretion is advised.

© A.K. Mitchell - The Crystal Code

Contents

MAP OF THE GEMFIELDS

N

RUBYVALE

SCRUB

RIDGE

BLACK
GATE

AUNT MAY'S
CIRCLE

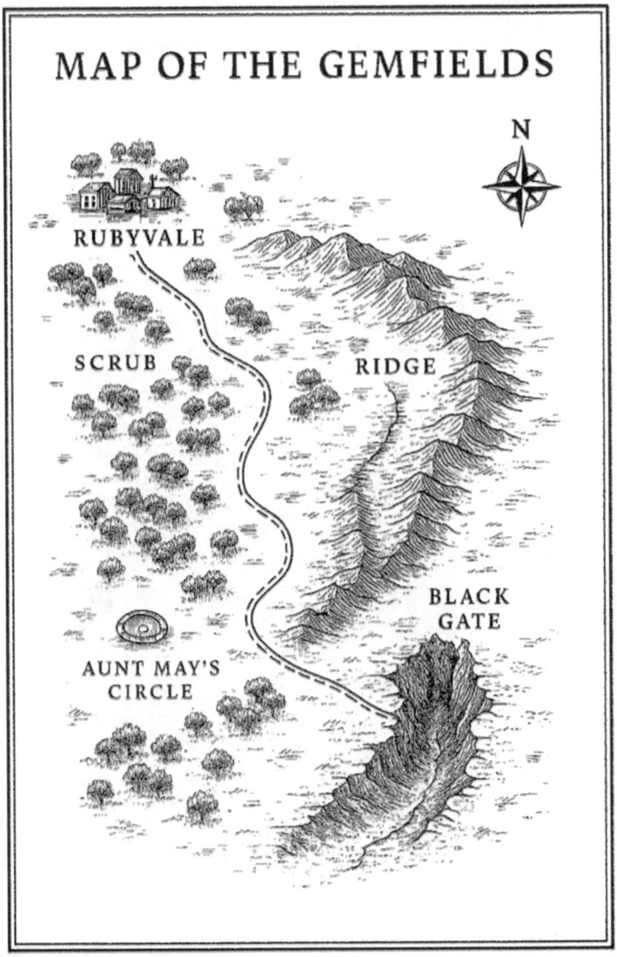

**Listen to the Crystal Code
Original Theme Song**

*Scan the QR code below or visit:
https://bit.ly/3XkgpCl*

*Composed by Mandikym
– from the forthcoming feature film adaption of The Crystal Code*

INTRODUCTION

T he Australian outback has always held secrets.
Beneath its vast skies and red earth lie stones that have
carried light for millions of years, sapphires formed in
silence and fire. Fossickers come chasing luck, miners
chasing fortune. Most find nothing. A few find beauty.
But sometimes, what is uncovered is not meant for
jewellery or trade. Sometimes, a stone is not a stone at all.

In Rubyvale, a struggling miner named Ella Fraser
uncovers a sapphire that hums with something more than
colour. When she touches it, the world hesitates: birds
freeze mid-flight, conversations repeat like bad
recordings, neighbours appear twice in the same place.
What begins as a whisper of strangeness grows into
fractures that ripple far beyond the Gemfields. Glitches
spreading throughout cities, skies, and lives across the
globe.

Drawn into the mystery are unlikely allies, a scientist
chasing patterns he cannot explain, an elder whose
stories remember truths older than science, and a
glitching stranger who insists Ella herself is not entirely
human. Around them, governments move in to seize and
weaponize what they cannot understand. At the heart of

it all is a question that will decide the fate of everyone. When reality reveals itself as code, do you reboot it clean...or override it, scars and all?

This is the story of stones that sing, of myths that prove more enduring than machines, and of one woman who discovers she may hold the key to the greatest choice ever offered to humanity.

01010010 01000101 01000010 01001111 01001111 01010100

CHAPTER ONE
RUBYVALE LIFE

The sun rose red over Rubyvale, painting the dirt roads and tin-roof shacks in a dusty glow. It was as if the whole town had been dipped in rust and left to bake. Ella knelt at the edge of her claim, fingers raw from another morning of shovelling gravel into the sieve. She shook the pan in a practiced rhythm, water sloshing like a miner's metronome as the heavy stones settled.

"Nothing. Just grit. Again," she sighed, brushing sweat from her forehead with the back of her arm.

"Every day's groundhog clay," she chimed. The Gemfields had a way of grinding people down, of turning weeks into years of the same hopeful motion; dig, sieve, wash, and pray for a spark of blue or green among the dust. Some called it a sickness, fossicker's fever. Ella just called it survival.

The days out here bled together: dust, diesel, sun, and hope, all in equal measure. You could tell the long termers by their hands: fingernails permanently black with dirt, knuckles cracked white and their skin tanned in stripes where gloves had once been. Mornings meant shovels and afternoons meant sorting through buckets of mud under tarps strung from old bed frames. Nights out here meant cheap rum and campfire stories that grew bigger every time the bottle got lighter. In The Gemmies, luck was a currency, and everyone swore they were only one shovelful away from changing everything.

⁎

Her generator coughed behind the shed, a sound between a death rattle and a smoker's laugh. The old beast was older than she was and was held together by duct tape, diesel, and denial. She'd meant to service it. But rates on the claim, food from the only general store in town, and fuel for the ute had eaten away the week's pay before it even began.

It had been her father's generator once. He'd given it to her when she first pegged the claim, swearing *'it had plenty of life left if you treat her right.'* And she believed him. Growing up on Moreton Island, that machine had powered plenty of family camping trips, sputtering to life every evening like a stubborn old aunt who refused to die quietly. Her father had always called it Jenny.

"Time to kick Jenny in the guts," he'd grin before yanking the cord. For years she'd wondered who Jenny was and what she'd done so wrong to deserve it. When she finally realised, she laughed so hard she nearly tipped the esky. Jennie had actually been Gennie, short for generator.

Now, standing in the dust and darkness, the memory almost made her smile. Almost. The generator sputtered again, the engine hiccupping in protest, and she gave it a half-hearted kick.

"Come on, Gennie," she pleaded.

"One more night."

The Gennie obliged with a groaning roar, the same rhythm she remembered from those island nights. It was the comforting thrum of a world that still made sense. But as the sound steadied, another hum seemed to rise beneath it. Lower and much stranger. Not diesel nor mechanical. It bled through the dirt and through the soles of her boots, until for a moment she couldn't tell which pulse belonged to the generator... and which belonged to the earth.

The claim wasn't much, just a patch of bush bordered by rusted drums and a caravan that too was much older than she was. A 1966 Travelhome, white once but now baked to silver, its corners sealed with layers of dust and stubborn faith. It had come from the next hill over, where it had sat unmoved for nearly thirty years, according to both its registration sticker and the collective memory of the locals. They said the old bloke who'd lived in it had pegged one of the earliest claims on

Bedford Hill and well, he never really left, not entirely.

The van came with him, in a way. Ella didn't believe in ghosts, but sometimes the cupboard door swung open by itself, slow and deliberate, like someone checking whether she'd eaten. Once or twice, a deck of cards she kept in the drawer turned up and it was if someone had already dealt two hands and lay waiting. It didn't bother her in the slightest. If anything, she found it comforting.

Inside, the walls still held the smell of old smoke and rust, and the wind carried red dust through every crack, no matter how many towels she stuffed under the door. The shower ran off a water pod that gave up by Friday, and the power came free from the sun when the panels decided to cooperate. Still, it was hers, a little slice of stubborn freedom carved from the bones of the earth.

One night, while rearranging her shelves, she'd found something that made her stop: scratched into the back of the bedroom wardrobe door was a faded mud map, part drawn in pencil and finger smudge and part looked to be burnt into the plywood. Bedford Hill claim was scrawled across the top in a hand that leaned left, with several X's scattered across the ridgeline. The sweet spots, the locals called them, the places the old timer had been chasing but never quiet reached. She'd traced the marks with her fingertip more than once, wondering if she was sleeping in the middle of a promise that still hadn't given up. A promise the land hadn't yet forgotten.

The old Travelhome had a few bullet holes through its front, leftovers from a story nobody really talked about. The previous owner's son, currently serving time for something Ella never asked about, had tried to disguise the damage years ago by plastering fake bullet-hole stickers across the van's panels. Unfortunately, the effort only made the real ones stand out more, the metal puckered and genuine beside the cartoon decals. It was both ridiculous and endearing, a kind of accidental honesty the Gemfields was full of. Despite all that, or maybe because of it, you could feel the quiet respect people had for the old van. It had survived weather, mischief, and whatever ghosts claimed it, and was still standing... and, well... same as the rest of them.

The sieve clinked, a scatter of ordinary pebbles that sounded like coins, only cruel ones.

"No change there," she said, tossing the useless stones to the ground staring out at the flat horizon that stretched endlessly like a desert screen stuck on repeat. Out here the world felt endless, yet sometimes she wondered if the world even rendered past the trees. It's like she could walk forever and never find the edge. And maybe that's what scared her: the thought that the world might have no edges at all, just an endless desert loop.

Across the gully, she could hear John's generator

coughing out the same rhythm as hers, followed by a string of swearing and the tinny crackle of the local radio station playing Slim Dusty on repeat. Someone farther up the track laughed, a deep belly sound that carried through the hills. Everyone worked alone out here, but nobody was ever truly alone. The bush had thin walls. Very thin walls.

Rubyvale wasn't a town so much as a suggestion. A scattering of shacks, caravans, and opportunists stitched together by dust and gossip. The post office doubled as a souvenir shop and the general store sold everything from diesel to divorce advice. Tourists came through in winter chasing the idea of adventure, bringing a sieve and a dream, then leaving by spring with sunburn and regret. But the ones who stay, the diggers, the dreamers, they had red dirt in their veins and no intention of ever leaving.

At noon she trudged to the pub. The New Royal sat squat by the highway like a relic half-remembered by time, its veranda sagging like a tired old dog and its ceiling fans spinning the air into slow regret.

The pub had been rebuilt years back to resemble the original New Royal that had burnt down sometime in the nineties, though no one ever agreed on what actually caused the fire. Some said it was faulty wiring. Others blamed a kerosene heater, or a bloke named Kev who *'meant well but had been on the rums.'* The new version was a log-wood affair, built to look rustic and old-worldly, which everyone found deeply ironic considering the first one had gone up in flames fast enough to roast a roo.

Still, it gave the town something to talk about for years. Feral Gemmies, red-eyed, dust-covered, and half-pickled would occasionally have too many before shouting fake threats they'd never follow through on.

'Should burn the bloody place down again!" someone would slur.

And everyone would laugh, because they all knew the truth… no one out here would dare. The pub was the heart of the place, and the heart was allowed to complain as long as it kept beating.

Ella remembered one miner, who'd been banned for starting a fight over a raffle. The next week, when they were taking entries for a chainsaw giveaway, the publican made him stand out front and make a solemn promise to the crowd:

'If you lot let me in the comp and I win the chainsaw," he'd said,

'I swear I won't get the shits and come back to cut the pub down."

The laughter had shaken the rafters, and he'd been let back in on the spot. Out here, that was what passed for a peace treaty and if it didn't, it stood out that you weren't from around here.

Rubyvale had even been in a movie once, a local claim to fame that still surfaced after a few drinks or anytime someone had had enough and thought about leaving. Ironically, the exact patch of dirt Ella had pegged for her claim was the very one featured in the film, well…one of the parts anyway. She hadn't known that for years, not until an old-timer pointed it out one night over rum. When she finally tracked down the film and watched it, she'd laughed out loud. The pub looked almost identical, right down to the old bar and the ceiling fans turning as slow as thoughts. The only real change was the missing Brisbane Bitter poster on the wall near the men's dunny. They didn't stock it anymore, but the memory of it still hung there like a ghost.

Travellers drifted through town every season, grey nomads chasing sunshine, backpackers chasing adventure and gem-hunters chasing the kind of luck that didn't exist anymore. Some ex-FIFO workers even came in dusty hire cars with maps printed off Google, expecting some kind of gold-rush romance but find only red dirt instead. Most stayed a night, maybe two, before realising that fossicking was a casual past-time and mining was mostly sweat, diesel, and disappointment. But a few never left. The Gemfields had a way of either catching people, holding them like a stubborn magnet or repelling them, never letting them back. Out here, you didn't just find stones, they find you.

Inside, the place smelled of spilt beer, dust, and nostalgia. A mix that could only be brewed by decades of sunburned mining stories. Mick stood behind the bar polishing a glass that was already clean, same as always, keeping one eye on the road in case another tourist wandered in looking for some fossickers luck or a bit of air-conditioning. He was as weathered as the hills, the kind of man with forty years of sapphire mining creased into his face.

"Anything today?" Mick called from the bar,

'Same as always," Ella muttered, dropping onto a bar stool.

'Dirt rich, sapphire poor."

He poured her a wine and lowered his voice.

"You hear about Old Tommy out near Reward? Swears he saw the ground shimmer like a heat haze. Next second his jackhammer stops dead. Wouldn't start again till the shimmer passed."

Ella raised an eyebrow.

"And…Equipment breaks all the time."

"Yeah, but this was different," Mick said.

'Said the bloody birds froze in the air. Just hung there, wings out, like statues. Then they dropped and flew off as if nothing had even happened."

She gave him a flat look.

"And just how many pints had Tommy had?"

Mick grinned.

"Enough...But not that many." They both chuckled in part dust, part disbelief.

"Maybe The Gemmies just needed buffering." Ella laughed,

"Happens to my phone every time I get anywhere near Reward."

Mick grinned, polishing a glass behind the bar as usual.

"Don't joke, love. Out here the Wi-Fi's bad enough without reality dropping out too."

The two of them laughed but neither mentioned how, lately, it wasn't just Wi-Fi that had started glitching.

When Ella first pegged her claim, the phone service was a joke. Half the time she didn't have reception at all, and when she did, it was only because she'd climbed up onto a stump, raised one leg like a drunken wallaby, and held her phone toward the sun at just the precise angle just to send a text. The locals swore there was a sweet spot out by the old mulga tree, one bar of service if the wind was right and you didn't breathe too hard. It was dubbed the unofficial phone box.

Even in town, it wasn't much better. Anyone at the

pub had to lean over the fence to make a call, shouting into their phones like true shipwreck survivors. The irony wasn't lost on anyone, the pub sat directly beneath the communications tower, but apparently the signal bounced right over it thanks to something the telco called the umbrella effect.

The TV was no better.

"TV Reception?" Mick had scoffed once to some out-of-towner who'd stopped in for the night.

"You'll need a VAST box and a satellite dish just to watch the bloody news 'round here."

Ella laughed, remembering the way it used to be. Out here, Wi-Fi was treated like witchcraft. You couldn't rely on the government, the weather, or your car battery, but if the Wi-Fi cut out, the whole town went feral.

Out here, gossip on the Rubyvale grapevine travels faster than the speed of light, but always much slower than the truth. Someone always knew someone who'd hit a pocket or seen a ghost. The Gemfields had its own folklore; stories traded over the bar like currency. And while most of it was nonsense, Ella sometimes wondered if the land remembered more than people gave it credit for.

The road shimmered under the setting sun as Ella walked home, her boots raising ghosts of dust behind her. The air still carried the smell of diesel and eucalyptus sap, that familiar outback perfume that clung to skin and memory alike. The cicadas screamed from the creek bed, their chorus thick and electric, pulsing with the last heat of the day. Out here, sunset didn't mean cool, it just meant the light changed colour.

Her muscles ached in that way they always did. The kind of ache that wasn't pain anymore, just the rhythm of work. She kicked at a bit of gravel and watched it tumble down the bank and vanish into the long grass. This was her favourite time: the lull between the noise of machines and the quiet that belonged to the bush. Usually, it calmed and grounded her. But this afternoon, something shifted.

It started out small, just a gap in the cicadas' song, then the faint pauses between gusts of wind. Then another. Then nothing. The air flattened. The light thickened. Even the dust seemed to hang in midair, waiting for something. She realised she couldn't even hear her own footsteps anymore. The dirt track, the trees, it was as if the whole bloody world had hit mute.

Even the flies, those uninvited saints of persistence had vanished. That alone was enough to unsettle her, as out here the flies never gave up. They were the true heartbeat of the place.

The silence wasn't empty; it had weight. She could

feel it pressing against her skin, the kind of stillness that makes you realise how loud you are just being in existence. She turned slowly, half-expecting to see someone…anyone…standing behind her. But nothing, no-one. Just red dirt and the bush that felt like it stretched on forever.

Then she noticed the light change and the shadows on the ground weren't moving anymore. Even the shimmer of heat seemed paused, frozen mid-wobble like hot glass that had forgotten how to melt. Her breath became shallow.

A kangaroo bounded across the ridge, then stopped. Not slowed, not faltered, stopped. Its body hung mid-leap, tail stiff, dust suspended in a perfect halo around it. The whole scene shimmered faintly, as though she were watching a paused video. For a second or two the air held its breath with her. Then just as sudden, the world snapped back. The sounds of the world crashed back in like a wave. The flies buzzed. The wind kicked up. The kangaroo landed, shook itself, and bounded off into the scrub like nothing had happened.

Ella stayed rooted to the spot and her heartbeat was hammering. The horizon rippled once more, faint but deliberate, as if the world was rebooting itself.

She swallowed hard, trying to steady her breath.

"Heat stroke," she explained to the empty dirt track.

"That's all." But her voice sounded strange, it was too sharp in the air, as though the silence hadn't fully left. She rubbed at her arms, the fine hairs still standing straight. The wind picked up again, but now it carried a different sound, a faint, almost electric hum, like the residue of a dream trying to remember itself. For a long while, she just stood there, hand shielding her eyes against the sinking sun, wondering whether it was the heat making her dizzy or something deeper.

Then, finally, she shook her head and walked.

"Or maybe it's just reality choking on a reboot," she said to amuse herself. But even as the words left her mouth, a generator coughed in the distance and the sound came a half-second too late.

That night, the air felt wrong, too still, too clean. Not a breath of wind pressed against the canvas awning. Even the moths seemed reluctant to move. Ella lay on her narrow caravan bed, one arm flung over her eyes. The single bulb above her buzzed, flickering just enough to remind her that power was never guaranteed. Each time it dimmed, she half-expected it wouldn't come back.

Moths threw themselves at the light like tiny prophets with poor aim, tapping against the shade in soft, frantic bursts. Outside, Stan's generator chugged with its usual uneven rhythm, but now every misfire sounded deliberate almost like punctuation in a sentence she couldn't read.

She turned onto her side, tracing the hairline cracks along the ceiling with her gaze. She'd done it a hundred times before, but tonight the cracks looked different. Longer maybe, or branching in new directions, as if they were growing toward something unseen. Her mind replayed the moment on the track, frame by frame: the shimmer, the frozen dust, the roo caught mid-leap. She told herself it was heatstroke. Mirages happened. Science could explain anything if you wanted it to.

She'd seen strange things in the bush before; heat mirages, storm fronts that never arrived, shadows that didn't belong to anything you could name. But this had been different. The stillness had felt deliberate, conscious, like the land itself had stopped breathing just to see if she'd notice.

'But still the way the world had stopped, utterly, like a computer between frames..." she exhaled. "

Stop thinking, El," she whispered.

"You'll go mad." But her brain didn't listen. It kept looping, debugging and searching for a missing line in the code of the day just gone.

She rolled onto her other side, staring through the flyscreen, out into the darkness. The horizon pulsed faintly under the half-moon light, a pale shimmer that could've been heat...or something else entirely.

Her father's old voice echoed in her head, the one that used to say,

'If you treat the land right, it'll treat you right back. Just don't go asking what it's thinking.' She smiled at the memory, but it didn't reach her eyes. Tonight, she couldn't shake the feeling the land had been...well, thinking and that it had thought of her.

*
**

The next morning, the sun rose red over Rubyvale, the same way it always did, as if the world hadn't noticed the glitch at all. Outside, the generator stuttered like a tired heart skipping beats, and for the first time, Ella wondered if the Gemfields held more than sapphires beneath its soil.

The wind rose, carrying the faint sound of laughter. Maybe Mick's, or maybe it was just her own echo. Then silence again. Ella knelt, shovel in hand. Same dirt. Same sieve. But when she sifted, the gravel seemed to shimmer, just for a moment as if something beneath was remembering how to be seen.

She looked up. The same bird traced the same arc across the sky, wing for wing. The horizon trembled faintly, like a smile that wasn't entirely friendly. And Ella, sun-burnt and dust-blown, laughed under her breath. "Guess I found another glitch," she said. "Or maybe..."

Her eyes flicked to the dust, shifting in perfect sync with her breath. "Maybe the glitch found me."

01000011 01001111 01000100 01000101

20

CHAPTER TWO
THE STRANGE SAPPHIRE

The morning sun came down like a hammer: hard and red. *"Less dawn and more detonation,"* Ella thought. She recalled the strangeness of the day before as the ground radiated yesterday's heat back through the soles of her boots. Already high, the sharp sunlight smacked the tin roofs and bounced off the dry dirt tracks. The world was already glowing like a frying pan full of regret.

Ella moved slower than usual with an ache behind her eyes that water wouldn't rinse away and skin tacky with heat. She told herself she hadn't seen what she'd seen. She told herself a lot of things out here.

"Morning sure hits different when it's still...well, last night," she groaned. The generator coughed a morning greeting that could double as an insult. Her shovel bit the tailings pile she'd been meaning to turn over for weeks with that dry metallic click that was half work, half confusion.

She set up at the wash trough, the gravel rasped into the sieve with a gritty, satisfying sound. Like rain...if rain had teeth. She dipped the pan in the trough and worked it in circles, letting the lighter sand bleed out in brown ribbons. The old rhythm steadied her. The miner's waltz: one-two-hope, then... maybe a flash of blue. Around and around. Settle the heavies. Tip away the fluff. A flash caught her eye. Not the usual mica gleam. Something much cooler. Deeper, with a pulse like a heartbeat under glass.

Back in the day, before tourists, TV shows and YouTube fossicking tutorials, newcomers would've never gone it alone like the newbies are doing now. You did an apprenticeship of sorts, years under the wing of an old-timer who'd seen enough dirt to know where the luck really lived. Some called them the Gemfields Patriarchs, though there were matriarchs too, tough old birds with hands like cracked stone and eyes that could spot a sapphire from fifty paces even if they were half blind.

These mentors taught more than just how to dig and wash; they taught survival, patience, and the quiet language of the ground. Where to camp, staying out of flood zones, how to read the shimmer in the wash, when to stop digging and just listen. They passed down trade secrets that weren't written anywhere. Not in maps, not in books. Things you only learned through red dust, bad whisky, and time.

And along with the miner's lore came the older lore, the Dreamtime stories Aunt May used to tell by the fire when Ella was a kid. Tales of stones that remembered the sky, of spirits that hid themselves in the earth until the right hands uncovered them. Out here, science and story blurred easy. The land didn't care what you believed, only whether you respected it.

Ella had a mentor once, a quiet old man who lived alone out near Reward, past an area that everyone called Jurassic Park. She guessed the name had stuck decades ago, when someone decided the jagged ridges and dry creek beds looked prehistoric in the afternoon light. Truth was, the area didn't look anything like the real Jurassic Park. Ella had seen the film's location herself once on a trip to Hawaii and remembered laughing at the comparison. Out here, the only dinosaurs were the LandCruisers still somehow running on hope and wire zip ties.

Her mentor, Frank, had been one of those men who spoke mostly in nods and grunts, yet could teach more in an hour than most could in a year. His claim was a quaint tin hut, mismatched panels, and the faint smell of diesel and eucalyptus.

She remembered sitting on the tailgate of his ute, boots swinging, as he pointed out the ridgelines and said,

"Ya don't look at the ground, Ya look through it. The sapphires are shy. You gotta make 'em feel seen, Ya see!" He'd shown her how to feel the wash through her fingertips, how to tell clay from promise, and how the

23

light sometimes bent differently when it struck the dirt hiding a gem.

"If you're meant to find it," he'd say,

"it'll find you right back." That was Gemfields wisdom in a nutshell, half folklore, half geology, and all faith. A place where the road names were jokes, landmarks were legends, and ambition came with a side of irony. There was a 3x5-foot timber lean-to down the hill grandly known as Buckingham Palace, a track you can't find named Whykickamoocow, and a bloody big spanner ready to tighten your nuts, should you ever start losing them. Yeah, this place had its unique quirks.

From Rubyvale to The Willows, each pocket of the Gemfields had its own quirks and its own map of humour and heartbreak. And somehow, through all the red dust and bad coffee, Ella had found her place among them.

Suddenly, Ella froze. She tilted the sieve. The flash winked again. Ella held her breath and eased two fingers through the wet gravel, feeling for edges. Her nail scraped something smooth. She worked the stone free and lifted it into the light.

It wasn't big as gems go, maybe the size of a thumbnail, but it had the unmistakable signatures of a sapphire, and a blue so clean it made her eyes sting.

Except the blue wasn't sitting still. It breathed. A soft pulse, like the surface was rippling from inside like it had a heartbeat and a secret.

As she turned it, threads of darker blue seemed to form and unform, mutating into neat grids that vanished before she could focus.

Ella glanced around without meaning to. No one. Just the wind dragging heat along the scrub, the flies orbiting, the trough gurgling. She set the stone on her palm, the skin there whitening with the cold she suddenly felt. She tilted it again. The blue shifted to gridlines that appeared, vanished, recompiled.

"Okay," she whispered to no one.

"That's...new." She closed her fingers around it firmly. The world stopped. Everything froze. The wash trough's water caught mid-splash, a fly suspended mid-buzz, sunlight itself looking suspiciously pixelated.

Ella began to wonder if this was the world holding its breath, or if it was somehow...buffering.

"Well, I guess reality is on dial-up today." Ella said aloud as if Mick could hear her, referring back to the Wi-Fi remark he had made yesterday at the pub. Unlike yesterday's hiccup, when the roo had stuttered through a moment. This was complete, like someone had pressed a cosmic pause button and every separate thing had agreed to obey.

The water in the trough arched in mid-splash, a glassy muscle frozen mid-contraction. A fly hung inches from her cheek, wings out like thin knives. The corrugated shade cloth over her wash station held a taut ripple that didn't finish rippling. Even the light itself felt...structured. Not just bright but arranged.

A sharp metallic taste rose on her tongue. The air smelled clean in a way that wasn't natural, like a room scrubbed of all scent. Her heart pounded too loudly in the silence, a drum in a tiny, sealed room.

When Ella opened her hand, the sound crashed back. Flies whining, generator chuffing three claims over, wind tugging the shade cloth until it finished its ripple and sagged. The water hit the trough with a slap that made her flinch.

She stood very still, the sapphire slick in her palm, breath going out in a long, shaky stream. Then she did the stupidest, most human thing: she tried again...Hand closing...Silence...Hand opening...Sound.

The third time, the frozen fly's eye caught the sun and threw a hard, perfect glint into hers. That broke whatever spell she was under. Ella wrapped the stone fast in the hem of her T-shirt and jammed it into the pocket of her cargo shorts, heart still sprinting.

She sat down hard on the edge of the trough, elbows on knees, hands clasped until the shake travelled out of them like a passing storm. The trough water slopped a little. The sky pretended it had always been just sky.

"All right," she told the red dirt.

'So that's real." A magpie laughed from the fence post like it was in on the joke. Her hand kept drifting to her pocket, but she stopped short each time.

"Not here. Not under the sun's security cameras." Ella warned the crystal. She kept working because that's what you do when the world turns strange: you just keep doing the next thing. Shovel, sieve, rinse. She found nothing else. Nothing but dumb gravel. Blessed, brain-dead stones. It should have disappointed her; instead, each one a tiny relief.

Every few minutes her hand drifted to her pocket, verifying the weight there, the cool press against her thigh. Each time, her fingers stopped short. Not here. Not out in the open.

By midday her shirt clung to her back and the horizon wobbled with heat. She covered the trough, stacked her tools, and headed for the caravan with her head down against the light. The path took her past Old Stan's rust-eaten Bedford truck. He sat in the shade beside it, eyes following her like they always did, beer in hand and grin welded on.

"You look like you saw a ghost, girl," he called.

"Just hot," Ella said. Stan tipped his hat.

"Heat does tricks. Keep your wits, girl. Or you'll start mining mirages."

She thought of the frozen fly's eye, her fist opening on a world resuming.

"Yeah," she said.

"I'm working on that." She kept walking. Behind her, Stan muttered something about reality tax being overdue. But as she walked, the thought wouldn't rest. What if it wasn't the heat? What if it was something else getting into her. Maybe the air, the water, the soil? She'd heard stories over the years…Everyone had…Rumours that when the film crew packed up decades ago, they'd dumped their leftover metal props and waste into the old pits. Lighting rigs, cables, and God-knows-what. Enough to poison a waterhole if the wrong chemicals were mixed in together, they say.

Then there were the darker tales. The ones that said the coal companies had been sneaking out here long before anyone knew, burying toxic runoff and waste drums in abandoned shafts to hide illegal mining or drive the sapphire diggers off their claims. No proof, of course. Never was. Just whispers that moved through the Gemfields like smoke.

After all, Rubyvale had earned its nickname and reputation fair and square. Rumourvale is what the local miners often called it. You couldn't separate truth from gossip out here even if you washed it ten times through the sieve. Still, the thought of radiation clung to her brain like red dust. Maybe it wasn't a glitch, maybe it was a leak, a sickness in the soil that's invisible and humming.

She touched her pocket again. The sapphire pressed cold against her skin, like it was waiting for her to decide which version of reality she wanted to believe.

Inside the caravan, the air was an oven. Ella kicked the fan alive, it sputtered awake like it was owed a favour. She crouched by the shallow drawer where she kept broken odds and ends. With a small screwdriver she levered the false bottom, just a flour bag glued to plywood, loose enough to slide the sapphire in. Then she lowered the panel, smoothed the bag, and set a stack of old mail on top. That automatic reaction to hide it made her frown and her stomach flip. *Really?* She thought, *Who exactly was she hiding it from?*

She drank some water, ran the tap until it coughed and spat, splashed her face then cut it before the pump protested. The mirror threw back a ghost with dirt freckles and existential hangover eyes. She certainly looked a shade or three paler than usual, hair clipped up in a plastic claw and a smear of dirt on her cheek she didn't bother to wipe.

Ella sat on the bed and stared at nothing until the nothing became something again. She tried to nap. The mattress springs pressed at familiar bruises, the fan pushed air over her knees, the caravan creaked as the day settled deeper into heat. Then suddenly, sleep slammed down hard like a trapdoor, the kind that doesn't begin gently so much as to drop a door between you and the world.

In her dream she stood in the middle of the scrub behind her claim. The sky above had been peeled back. Beneath the luminous blue was a lattice, clean as graph paper and as bright as an afterimage, stretching in every direction until it meets itself. She could see right through it, she could see the ground and the trees and her own body, but the lattice held primacy, the way a wireframe model holds a shape before the skin is rendered. The world rendered in geometry.

It flickered like a glitching neon light. And in that moment, she understood. Not with words but with certainty, that the flicker was representing time.

Suddenly, a figure moved at the edge of the field. For a moment she thought it was her father. Ridiculous, impossible, he'd been gone for years but the gait wasn't right, and the shadow didn't stick to the ground properly. It appeared half-formed and flickering. It stepped closer and its outline stuttered between two positions, like a badly synced video feed.

The air went still again. The shadow hesitated at the boundary of her claim, head tilted as though watching her. Then, as quick as a thought, it was gone, not vanished, exactly, but folded into the light, leaving only a faint shimmer that refused to settle.

Ella let out the breath she hadn't realised she was holding. Out on The Gemmies, people told stories about the Shadows of the Gemfields, old folklore whispered around campfires and passed down like miners' prayers. They said the shadows watched over every stone, keeping count of what the earth gave and what it took back. They protected the gems from greed and punished those who dug with more hunger than heart.

Old-timers claimed the shadows weren't ghosts but keepers of stone. The spirits of those who'd dug before, bound to the veins of sapphire that had fed them in life. They moved at dusk, between shifts of light, half in the world and half in whatever lay beneath it.

"The stones remember," Aunt May had always said, poking at the fire until sparks jumped.

"They remember who digs honest and who digs hungry." Most miners laughed off the tales, that was until their gear went missing, or their pumps clogged for no reason, or the ground collapsed without warning. Then

31

they'd go quiet, whisper an apology to the dirt, and some are said to pour a shot of rum into the soil before starting work again. A peace offering, just in case the shadows were listening.

Ella wasn't superstitious, or so she liked to think. But standing there, skin prickling, she couldn't shake the feeling that something had taken notice.

"Don't," it said. Or maybe it said,

"Do." The voice arrived off-timed, half a beat late.

"Keys," it said, or

"Nodes," or

"Home." Each word landed on the wrong frame. Ella reached up and curled her fingers in the air. The lattice bulged under her touch the way a drum skin dips. She pushed harder. The grid dented around her hand, a beautiful elastic moan of the universe stretching. The lines stretched out and nodes brightened where they met. A sound like a chord rang out, strained at the point of pressure, halfway between music and math. A beautiful, almost-familiar interval at the edge of breaking.

She let go. The grid snapped flat with a sound like a whip in an empty room. The figure flickered, hand raised toward her in something like a warning or maybe a greeting. Then silence.

She woke gasping, mouth metallic and brain electric. The fan rattled.

"Dreams with frame rates," she said.

"I must be losing it."

✲

The knife of afternoon light through the caravan window had shifted. Outside, a ute rattled past on the track, rolling a lazy dust ghost behind it. Ella sat up slowly, stretched, and rubbed her hands over her face until stars danced behind her eyelids.

She didn't dream much anymore. Not like that. Not with structure.

The memory of the lattice hung clear as if she'd drawn it on the air with a stick. She reached for the drawer before she could talk herself out of it, slid the false bottom back, and lifted the sapphire like it might protest.

In her palm it pulsed once, a slow inhale of light. Ella swallowed.

"Okay," she said softly.

"Let's see you out in the sun." She took it outside and held it where the shade thinned. Sunlight saturated the blue into something so dense it felt heavy. Little fractures inside it. No, not fractures…Paths…Threads.

Every miner knew that sunlight told the truth of a stone. You held it up and turned it slowly, letting the light slide through to reveal its story, its colour, clarity, and if it contained any cracks. You looked for silk lines,

33

those faint internal wisps that made a gem softer to the eye but weaker to the wheel. Too many cracks and it was just a cutter's heartbreak. Too few and it was a keeper, a stone born whole. Most miners held them up toward the sun the way priests hold relics, reverent and hopeful while pretending not to pray.

Frank had taught her that. She could still see him standing beside the wash trough, holding a rough blue chip between thumb and forefinger.

'Don't just look at it," he'd said.

'You gotta let the light do the talking. Tilt it, listen. The stone'll tell you what it's made of and what it's hiding." He'd turned the gem just so, sunlight bending through it in clean, silent syllables.

'There. See that pale band? That's its fault line. Every stone's got one. You just hope yours doesn't run too deep." He'd smiled then with that half-smile he used when he was saying something bigger than the words themselves.

'People and stones, love. We're all full of cracks. The trick's finding the ones that still shine through." The memory warmed her even now. Only this stone's light didn't just shine, it moved. It folded and breathed, like a pattern tracing through its heart echoing circuitry awakening after a long sleep.

Ella tilted it between her fingers, watching the light run its examination. The blue deepened until it seemed to drink the sunlight itself. Inside, something shimmered, not just the usual refraction but motion, like a light trapped inside a maze that was learning its own exits.

When she tilted the stone, for a fraction of a second, the threads aligned into a neat crosshatch like tiny corridors, intersections or a crystalline city under construction. They then dissolved into chaos again.

She pressed the pad of her thumb to the stone, and the skin there went numb with cold, the cold racing up her arm like a mouthful of winter. She closed her fingers, half-expecting the world to freeze again.

Nothing happened.

She frowned. Kept her hand closed another beat. The flies stayed flies, the wind made tiny dunes on the dust. She opened her hand. The stone sat as innocently as a bead from a child's bracelet.

'So, you decide when, bloody drama queen,' she said to it, and immediately felt stupid for saying anything at all.

From the ridgeline: voices. Men's. Crisp. Imported. Not the casual slope-shouldered voices of locals. Tighter and more clipped. Ella slipped the sapphire back into her pocket, the cool weight of it, a brand against her thigh.

She stepped to the side of the caravan to see without being seen.

Two figures came down the track in sun-bleached uniforms that hadn't started out that colour. One carried a metal case dressed in researcher chic; the other wore sunglasses you couldn't buy in Emerald. They were smiling, the way people smile when they've already decided you're going to agree.

"Afternoon," Sunglasses called when they saw her.

"Hot one."

"Always," Ella said. Her hand hovered near her pocket, then decided not to hover.

"We're doing a bit of a survey," he said, tapping his case.

"University connection. Geological anomalies out this way. You heard anything unusual? Lights, vibrations, strange readings?" The smile sharpened.

"Found anything interesting yourself?" His partner unfolded a brochure like this was a sausage sizzle fundraiser. Ella didn't look at it. She looked at their boots. New. No red dust crusted in the seams. She looked at their hands. No thin crescent scars on the knuckles from sieves, no nail beds permanently black with dirt.

"Only strange thing I've seen today is optimism. Rare mineral round here." They laughed politely, not catching

the barb. Their boots were too clean. Their eyes, too
rehearsed.

'Seriously though, the only interesting thing around
here today was a flat tyre on Mick's ute,' she said.

"You can log that." They chuckled like she'd made a
little joke at a party. Sunglasses nodded at the trough and
the tailings.

'We'll just take a quick look around. Purely optional,
of course."

"Then that'll be a solid no," Ella said pleasantly.

"After all, optional is my favourite kind of no." They
did a little dance of politeness and patience, then
retreated with promises to be back with real forms and
proper words after discovering that without a formal
induction, they can't just walk onto a mining claim like
they can a residential property. She watched them go
until the heat shimmer ate them. Only then did she
realise her fingertips had been tingling the whole time.

She went back inside and locked the door, a ridiculous
gesture out here and therefore, perhaps, the only one that
mattered. With the door locked and the fan whining, her
hand shook as she laid the sapphire on the table. Inside
it, she could see the tiny worlds moving inside it. Lines
wove and unwove, and grids folding like origami in
reverse that refused to be stable.

37

Keys, the dream figure had said, or nodes...maybe home. Ella thought as she sat in confusion. Just like the sky in the dream and the frozen fly and the moment the world remembered to breathe.

She touched the stone with one finger, gentle as a prayer. The caravan shivered. Not a sway or a creak, those shivers she knew well, but this shiver was like it was running through matter, as though every screw and rivet had just discovered it was made of math. The fan hiccuped then resumed. Outside, a single magpie note stretched too long, a wire pulled tight.

Ella jerked her hand away. The shiver stopped. Air flooded back into the room as if it had been waiting at the door. Her laugh came out wrong, and she clapped a hand over her mouth to pin it down.

"All right," she whispered.

"You're not just a rock." The light shifted again, the day collapsing toward evening. The ridgeline went gold then brass then dull. Somewhere a generator coughed into life, a sound like someone trying to keep the world turning by will alone.

Ella wrapped the sapphire in a strip of old pillowcase and slid it back into its hiding place. She palmed the drawer shut and stood there, listening to the caravan talk to itself, the tin, wood, wire, all of it settling into the night's version of the same shape.

She washed her face in a bowl, changed her shirt, and sat at the little table. She took a pen and the back of an unpaid bill and drew what she remembered: a grid, a bulge where her hand had dented it, nodes bright at the corners. When she lifted the pen, the lines seemed to hum on the paper as though they wanted to keep going, to complete a picture she couldn't yet see.

When she turned out the light and lay down on her bed, she didn't pray. She didn't bargain. She stared into the dark and tried to count backwards from a hundred...It didn't help. The numbers wanted to repeat.

Sometime soon after, the night finally took her, the sapphire under the drawer pulsed once, just once, blue washing through blue like it took a breath. And outside, in the space of a single skipped heartbeat, the stars arranged themselves into a lattice so precise that any God or programmer watching might have smiled.

01010100 01101000 01100101 00100000 01000011 01110010 01111001 01110011
01110100 01100001 01101100 00100000 01000011 01101111 01100100 01100101

CHAPTER THREE
THE SCIENTIST ARRIVES

The next morning, Ella woke to the sound of tyres crunching on gravel, a sound so foreign it feels like punctuation in the middle of silence. Out here, you always knew when someone new arrived. The track behind her claim hardly ever saw strangers, not unless they were lost, or selling something, or both. One of them wound up the back ridge like a lazy scar, leading eventually to what the locals still called the airstrip.

Ella was convinced it hadn't seen a landing since the filming days back in the eighties, when the movie crew had touched down there in a rickety charter plane full of equipment and too much optimism. These days it was just a long, sun-cracked scar of clay and weed, reclaimed by spinifex for half a year and track half-swallowed by time. Sometimes kids rode motorbikes along those tracks until either the fuel or their courage ran out.

The old airstrip doubled as Ella's fifth, or maybe sixth access track. She'd lost count years ago. Back when she was first hunting for a patch to peg, multiple access points had been one of the unspoken criteria an old-timer had told her. You never wanted just one way in or out of your claim, not out here. Floods, fires, busted engines, or a blue with a neighbour could turn a single track into a trap.

Ella had that many tracks now that she could take a different one home every day for a week and never cross her own tyre marks. The only other people who knew those back routes as well as she did were the bikers, the dirt riders who tore through on weekends mostly. In winter when the ground went hard and the air tasted like metal, you'd sometimes hear the echo of engines up that way. A hum so distant and ghostly it drifted over the sound of miners cutting wood for their fires or just getting themselves half-lost before dark. Not many ventured too far in, though. A maze of old ridge roads twisting back on itself. And then there were the stories…everyone had heard them…about people who'd gone up and never came back. Out there, even the GPS gave up, and the land had its own ideas about direction.

Sometimes, when the wind came from the west, Ella swore she could hear the hum of an old Cessna engine out by the airstrip, steady, low, and looping, as though an old plane were forever trying to take off or something. She stepped out of the caravan with a mug of inspiration, squinting against the morning glare on multiple

42

occasions, only to find it was a Gennie off in the distance that was also trying to start its day.

*
**

A white Land Cruiser idled by near her fence line, dust ghosting around its tyres. Out stepped a man in a collared shirt too clean for the Gemfields, sleeves rolled neatly, notebook tucked under one arm. His boots looked new, but at least they'd had the courtesy to meet some dirt as he scuffed them on the walk down the hill toward Ella's claim.

She took a slow sip of the coffee, grimaced at the bitterness, and concluded:

"Not a local, then." The Land Cruiser's engine ticked as it cooled. The man paused at her gate. He'd hesitated, as though uncertain whether to walk in and knock or call out, then raised a polite hand in greeting.

"Morning," he said, voice steady but formal, the kind that carried university corridors in its vowels.

"Ella Fraser?" he asked.

"Who's asking?" she replied, stepping out onto the dirt, dressing gown catching at her knees. He held up an ID wallet, something with a crest she didn't recognise...a university...or government department perhaps. Either way, something that looked smugly coastal.

"Dr. Kael Nathan. Mineral physics. I've been seconded to a survey project in the region." He offered a small, precise smile.

"I hear you've had some interesting finds." Ella eyed him over the rim of her mug, leaning against the doorframe.

"That depends on who's asking and what they mean by interesting." Kael's smile didn't quite reach his eyes. It was the kind that makes instruments nervous. Her hand twitched toward her pocket automatically, where the sapphire pulsed against her thigh like a kept secret. She forced herself still.

"Plenty of people find things out here. Rocks, mostly, sapphires sometimes." She went on and Kael chuckled softly, as though they'd shared a private joke.

"I'd love to take a quick look at your wash plant. Purely academic curiosity, of course."

"Yeah, it seems there's a lot of curiosity around lately," Ella said.

"Curiosity tends to pay better when it's buying the beer." Her tone was sharper than she meant, but sarcasm was easier to reach for than trust. He studied her a moment, first in the professional way, the way scientists measure things they've already decided how to catalogue and then, briefly, differently. His gaze lingered just a second too long, long enough for her to feel the warmth of it before he looked away.

It had been a long time since she'd had a man look at her that way... or in any way, really. Out here, life didn't leave much room for that sort of thing. Men came and went through the Gemfields like weather fronts: hot, unpredictable, and usually gone by morning. She'd had someone once, a few years back. Thought he'd stay. But the Gemfields has a way of stripping people down to their essentials, and some didn't like what they found underneath.

He'd lasted a wet season and half a dry before packing up his ute and heading back to the city, claiming he needed *real work* and *proper Wi-Fi*. She'd never argued. She couldn't compete with the comfort or convenience that city life offers.

Sometimes, though, when the nights dragged on and the only sound was the generator coughing behind the shed, she missed the simple company. Not the romance but the presence. Someone to hand her a spanner or share a wine under the sky so big it makes us feel smaller in a good way.

Now here was Kael, too neat, too curious, too educated for this place and here he was standing in her dust, like he belonged there. And damned if that didn't stir something she'd buried under practicality and diesel fumes.

He snapped his notebook shut. The sound made her flinch more than she meant it to.

"I'll be around," he said, voice calm, careful.

"If you change your mind," He offered then nodded toward the ridgeline.

"Things are happening out here, Ms. Fraser. Things bigger than sapphire mining."

She watched his Land Cruiser trail dust toward town, unsettled by how quickly he'd zeroed in on her and by how much she wanted him to. The sapphire throbbed once in her pocket, as if agreeing with her thoughts.

That afternoon, Ella took her sieve to a creek bed farther up from the dirt track that trekked past her claim. She didn't want eyes on her while she worked. She dunked the sieve into the shallow water that was whispering secrets over her boots when a soft cough interrupts the rhythm.

An old woman stood beneath the shade of a bloodwood tree, wrapped in a faded scarf. Her eyes sharp as flint. It was Aunt May, one of the local elders. Ella was more used to seeing her outside the store these days. Sometimes telling stories to the kids, and sometimes just staring out at nothing with all the weight of the years on her shoulders.

"You found one," Aunt May said simply, but not as a

question.

Ella froze, sieve half-shaken.

"Found one what?" Aunt May stepped closer, barefoot grace on burning red dust. She moved with a steadiness that made the land want to lean with her. It was like the air around her was slightly mis-aligned, as though reality's grid forgot to pin her properly.

"A stone that sings." Aunt May replied.

"They are not new, my dear. They were here long before us, long before the Dreamtime stories were first told. We say they hold the songs of creation." Ella blinked. The words tugged at something old and half-buried.

She tried to remember the stories she'd been told as a kid visiting the Gemfields on school holidays, her mother letting her sieve through the wash while Aunt May spoke in that calm, knowing voice that made the campfire seem older than it was. There had been talk of song-stones, of blue hearts that hummed when the ground was listening, of miners who'd heard whispers through their sieves on windless nights. She'd believed it once. She remembered that much.

But the rest was gone, wiped clean, the way the earth forgets footprints after rain. She couldn't recall what she'd found back then, or if she'd found anything at all. Only that the air had felt charged, like a storm deciding whether to strike. Ella felt her mouth go dry.

"Umm... It's just a sapphire." Aunt May's eyes held hers, unwavering.

'Some sapphires are doors. My dear Ella," she tapped her temple.

"And some of us can hear when they open." The air between them shimmered for a moment, not heat shimmer, but something subtler, as if the edges of Aunt May's body flickered between two outlines. Ella blinked hard, and it was gone.

The old woman turned without another word and walked back toward the ridge, her figure shrinking into the rippling horizon. Ella stared down at the sieve. The gravel seemed ordinary enough, but when she tilted it, for just a heartbeat the stones inside formed a neat little grid perfect, mathematical, deliberate. Then the water sloshed, and it was gone. She blinked hard, the pattern lingering behind her eyes like the afterimage of lightning.

'Get a grip," she told herself, shaking the pan once more. But the rhythm was gone now. The miner's waltz had turned into static.

By sunset, she was back at the caravan...she'd packed up early. The air felt wrong, it was just too still...too clear. And she couldn't shake the sense that the ground was holding its breath again.

She lit the lamp, poured the dregs of her wine, and watched moths spiral around the glass chimney. Their wings flickered in and out of the glow, each one a glitch of its own. She set the sapphire on the bench. Even under lamplight, it pulsed faintly, the blue deep and calm, like it knew things she didn't. Outside, the generator's uneven cough became a steady hum. It sounded smooth, precise... almost mechanical perfection. That should have comforted her. Instead, it made her skin crawl.

The night pressed in close. Through the window, the stars scattered sharp and unreal over the black horizon, too bright, too evenly spaced. Out beyond the claim, the old airstrip cut a pale scar through the scrub, and for a moment, she thought she saw something moving along it. Just a flicker of light, too slow for a car, too fast for a person. She stood there watching until it disappeared into the darkness, her reflection superimposed against the glass, a ghost in her own window.

"Heat shimmer," she told herself.

"That's all." But when she lay down, the hum followed her into sleep.

That night, she dreamed again of the luminous blue lattice sky. Only this time, she wasn't alone. Dr. Kael Nathan stood beside her in the dream, pen poised over his notebook, smiling right at her, as if he'd been waiting there all along. Around them, the stars rearranged themselves in neat lines forming grids, grids forming shapes, and shapes that pulsed like breathing.

"See it?" he asked, voice calm, steady.

"I don't know what I'm seeing," she whispered.

"It's not seeing," he said softly.

"It's remembering." The lattice rippled, and the sound it made wasn't sound at all, it was code, sung through light. The sapphire in her dream had glowed until it actually became the sky itself, infinite and alive.

When she woke up, the caravan light was still on. The sapphire on the bench pulsed once, faint but deliberate, and the 12-volt fan hummed in perfect, unbroken rhythm.

Ella sat up, heart pounding. The night outside was silent except for the faintest echo, somewhere far off, of a man's voice carried on the wind. She couldn't make out the words, but she knew the tone. Curious. Certain. It was Kael's.

She couldn't sleep. The air inside the caravan was thick with the smell of hot tin and old fabric softener, the kind that clung to everything no matter how many times she washed it. Outside, the crickets sang their endless chorus, and inside the fan whined in its usual rhythm.

She poured herself another splash of wine. Cheap, warm, and mostly vinegar by now. She sat by the narrow window, watching the faint glow of town far off across the hills. It was barely a cluster of lights, more of a memory than a civilisation, but it was enough to remind her that she wasn't completely alone out here. Not yet, anyway.

She caught herself thinking about him, Dr. Kael Nathan and the way he'd stood, all straight lines and calculation. He carried the faint smell of aftershave that didn't belong out here. Not the harsh stuff the miners wore, but something clean, almost clinical. A scent that said city, civilisation, and order. She hated herself a little for noticing and for caring.

It had been years since she'd let anyone into her personal space, years since she'd shared a bed that wasn't built into a caravan frame or surrounded by red dust. The Gemfields had its own rhythm, one that didn't sync well with love or company. People had always seemed to pass through, not into, her life.

She traced the rim of her glass, watching the moonlight pool inside it. The sapphire pulsed once from where it sat wrapped in cloth on the benchtop, a faint electric blue ghost.

"Don't start," she pleaded to it.

"I've already got one mystery to figure out."

Outside, the motor on Stan's trommel coughed once, twice, then settled into a steady hum, only it was too steady and too even. The same unnatural precision she'd started to notice in everything around The Gemfields lately.

Ella stared out the window, her reflection merging with the night beyond. Was she just one woman caught between dust and data, watching the darkness watching her right back?

Again, once she'd finally resettled, she returned to the dream of the luminous blue lattice sky. Again, she wasn't alone. Kael stood beside her, pen poised over his notebook, smiling right at her, as if he'd been expecting her to return to the dream.

01000100 01010010 01000101 01000001 01001101

03:14 – Wind stops simultaneously across four sensors.

0 Hz 53Hz 106Hz 159Hz

Audio spectrogram shows 53 Hz carrier with harmonic ladder at 106/159 Hz.
"Not "silence" it's attention."
Note to self:
language matters.

CHAPTER FOUR
CRACKS IN REALITY

By late morning the heat had set in. It had teeth today, the kind that bites through both canvas and patience, metal pings when you touch it, and the air tastes like static. Ella worked in the narrow strip of shade cast by the caravan, sweat shining on her burned shoulders and her eyes stinging from the glare.

She'd moved the sapphire from the drawer to a cloth pouch she could hang around her neck under her shirt. The weight was small, relentless. Every move reminded her of it.

She rinsed a sieve of tailings and found nothing but ordinary disappointment. When she looked up, old Mrs. Dalloway waved from the top track, a plastic grocery bag swinging from her wrist. Mrs. Dalloway lived in a donga two claims over and was always bringing people things they hadn't asked for. Jam jars. Newspaper clippings about floods from ten years ago. Scones that tasted like they'd been baked by a memory. She tottered down the track, waving the plastic grocery bag like a peace flag.

"Morning, love!" she called.

"You want lemons? Tree's gone mad."

"Sure," Ella said, wiping her hands on her shorts. Mrs. Dalloway's smile spread the same way sunlight spreads across an old tin roof...bright and careless. She stepped closer and the bag rustled.

Without warning, a second Mrs. Dalloway walked into view from behind the caravan. Same hat, same bag, same smile. She turned the corner and there they were: two old women, identical down to the crease where the hat brim had been folded once too many times. Both women paused, both smiled wider, both lifted the bag at the same angle. And then, like someone finished a thought and moved on, one of them blinked out of existence. Not gone so much as never there. The remaining Mrs. Dalloway continued, oblivious.

Ella's throat went dry. She glanced at the ground where the duplicate had been; the dust held only one set of shoe scuffs. The old woman pressed lemons into Ella's hands, heavy and real.

"Bit hot today," Mrs. Dalloway said cheerfully, handing over lemons the size of an average man's fists.

"You look pale, dear."

"I'm fine," Ella said, voice thin.

"Thank you."

"Put them in water a spell. Makes the skin come right off." The old woman squinted at the sky.

"Funny light, I might say."

"Yeah," Ella said. "Very funny light."

When she was alone again, she set the lemons on the table and pressed her palms into the metal on the kitchen sink until the sharpness of heat cut through the tremor in her hands. The world felt under-proofed, not quite baked. She pulled the pouch from under her shirt and stared at the fabric, as if it might confess to something. The stone inside felt cool through the cloth. It always felt cool.

"Okay. Proof. Need proof." She said to the stone.

"Not stories. Not a roo hung mid-air like a sick Halloween joke. Not a disappearing neighbour. Something I can measure." Even if only by saying the word measure out loud was daring the world to disagree with her.

Ella knelt by her makeshift workstation. A tin bucket, stopwatch, and her phone recording on a shaky tripod. The strange sapphire sat in her palm, cool, inert, and seemingly far too calm for something that had stopped the world only yesterday.

"Alright, Bluey," she said.

"Let's see if lightning strikes twice or if you were just showing off." Ella taped the stopwatch…The phone screen flickers once…then stabilises. A breeze passes…or maybe it doesn't. Even the flies hesitate mid-buzz.

A shimmer rolls across the dirt, bending the light like heat haze. Ella squints: her reflection in the bucket ripples, fractures, then reassembles slightly offbeat as if her image forgot its line in the script.

"Okay," she whispers,

"that's not normal. Not even Gemfields-normal." Her voice trembles but her grin doesn't. There's a glint of scientific curiosity in her eyes, one part wonder, two parts stubborn defiance. This was just far too much to take in first thing in the morning, perhaps she should've had another coffee before starting the day.

She steadies the sapphire on the dirt, aligns the shadow, and hums under her breath, a tune her mother used to sing while sieving gold in the creek beds around the old ghost-town of Pratten, long before they had a $1 land sale, which saw the weathered, time-worn town come buzzing back to life. The sound seems to anchor the air. Then…Click…The stopwatch freezes…So does everything else.

The breeze halts mid-whisper. A speck of dust hangs suspended between her fingers like a caught pixel. Ella blinks once and the world stays perfectly still.

"Guess time's got stage fright," she says softly. Her laugh sounded strange in the silence, too loud, too separate. She waves a hand through the air. Light fractures like glass, around it, every motion echoing behind her as if faint afterimages. She exhales and sets the sapphire down. It seemed as though the world had exhaled with her. Flies resume flying, dust falls, and sound rushes back, filling the air like applause after a long pause.

Ella glances at the phone camera, still recording. The timer on the screen is wrong. It's off by several seconds. She rewinds the clip, scrubs through the moment of the freeze, and frowns. In the playback, she vanishes completely for three frames.

"Well," she murmurs,

"That's one way to lose track of yourself." A half-smile, half-grimace. It was perfectly normal to lose track of time, as time drifts differently out here on the Gemfields. Out here, days blurred into dust and sunlight. But come Friday, it was like every Gemmie felt it in their bones…time to head to the pub for the pub card draw. She presses stop, pockets the sapphire, and looks to the horizon where the light flickers again. It really was as if reality itself is blinking.

Ella needed to clear her head, the strangeness was getting all a bit too much. She took the hand trowel and walked to the far cut-out, past Old Stan's truck where the scrub thinned and the dirt went hard and pale. Here the ground had a way of ringing when you stomped, a faint hollow that made miners go quiet and listen for luck.

Out on the Gemfields, fortune didn't shine, it murmured. A single wrong step could drop a fool into a forgotten shaft, the earth swallowing them whole before they even have time to swear. Yet the same hollow sound could mean something else entirely: the promise of a sapphire pocket waiting just beneath the crust, light trapped in darkness for a million years. The difference between falling and finding was often less than an inch and in Rubyvale, that inch was the layer where both Gods and glitches liked to hide.

Ella worked her boot heel into the crust. Dust hopped obediently away from the pressure and settled in a soft sigh. She knelt and scraped back a shallow trench with the trowel. Red dirt, more red dirt, a hard layer, then... she stopped. The trowel clicked against something that didn't sound like rock.

She cleared more. A plate of some kind, maybe...or something else...it was smooth and dark and laying just beneath the soil, the size of a dinner tray, edges too straight to be natural. Metal was the information her brain provided. But whatever it was, it didn't reflect. Even in the hard noon light it seemed to drink brightness, its surface absorbing and resolving into nothing. Along one edge, the faintest grid of lines ghosted into being when she leaned closer…like condensation on glass. Then gone. Ella's breath fluttered.

She touched the metallic-looking plate with two fingers. For a moment, the ground around her flickered frantically. The prickle-bush at the edge of her vision split into two possible bushes, then chose one. The air brightened and dimmed and took a moment to decide which way it had always been.

Ella jerked her hand away and rocked back on her heels. The plate-like object lay dumb and blank as if she'd imagined the grid she had just seen.

"Not just rocks," she mused when suddenly, behind her, someone cleared a throat in a deliberate manner.

She spun, heart in her throat, unsure of what to expect. She breathed a sigh of relief when she saw it was Kael, who stood no more than ten metres away, hands raised as if approaching a skittish horse. His shirt had creases ironed into them, which Ella took as an insult to the day. He looked past her at the shallow open-cut, then down at the ground, as if the earth might answer a question that he didn't want to ask in front of her.

"You should be careful where you dig," Kael eventually said.

"I am careful," Ella snapped back, more sharply than she intended.

He crouched beside the open-cut pit while keeping a

polite distance. The air between them shimmered faintly in the heat or maybe it wasn't just the heat.

"May I?" he asked, nodding toward the hole Ella was working.

"No," she automatically said, then sighed.

"Fine. But don't…just don't touch it."

Kael smiled faintly, that scientist's smile that wasn't about people at all, it was the kind that meant his mind was already somewhere deep underground, racing ahead of the conversation.

"Noted," he said.

He leaned closer, bracing one hand on his knee as he peered into the shadowed layer of stone. The veins of luminous blue light caught his eye, and for a moment his composure slipped. His breath hitched, barely audible. But Ella caught it.

"What?" she asked. Kael hesitated just a little too long.

"It's…unusual." He swallowed.

"You found one."

"One what?" She quizzed. He glanced around, as if he were checking the air for microphones, then lowered his voice.

"Something we've been…tracking…Quietly."

"Tracking?" asked Ella. He exhaled, clearly torn between protocol and something more personal.

"Let's just say this...whatever it is...it has shown up in data before. But never in person." His gaze flicked to her, then quickly away.

"You shouldn't even be standing this close to it." Ella folded her arms.

"That's comforting," she said rolling her eyes. He gave a soft, distracted laugh, the kind that wasn't really laughter at all.

"Sorry. I don't mean dangerous. Just... responsive."

"Responsive?" she asked. Kael straightened, brushing the dirt from his palms, eyes darting to the horizon like he'd already said too much.

"I shouldn't be talking about this."

"Then don't," Ella said. But part of her didn't want him to stop. He hesitated again, studying her. Not the claim. Not the rock. Her. His eyes were sharp, analytical but there was something else there too. A flicker of something...human.

"When you touched it," he asked quietly,

"did anything change?"

Ella's throat went dry. She thought of the air freezing, of the world stuttering like a bad video file. But she wasn't about to hand him that.

"Define change," she asked carefully. He gave a ghost of a smile.

"That's what I'm trying to do."

A gust of wind swept through the cut, stirring the red dust between them. Kael looked down, watching it swirl around his boots. Then he said, almost under his breath;

"They call it an interface. That's what the models suggest, anyway. But between what and what…" He trailed off, shaking his head.

"That part doesn't translate."

"You're speaking in riddles." Ella frowned.

"I know." His voice softened.

"It's safer that way. Trust me." The space between them pulsed with quiet tension. She was aware of the sweat trickling down her spine, the smell of diesel and dust, and the faint clean scent of his aftershave that didn't belong out here.

Kael stepped back, forcing a polite smile.

"Look, maybe I shouldn't have said anything. I'm not allowed so forget it. Forget I came by."

"Yeah? Well…Bit late for that, isn't it?" she said.

He nodded once, like a man making a decision he didn't like.

"All right, then. Let me buy you a drink tonight. The New Royal. Early. Before all the noise starts."

She arched an eyebrow.

"Why?"

"Because," he said quietly, "you look like someone who's seen something they're not sure they should have. And if I'm right, you look like the type of person who wants to choose who hears about it."

Ella almost said no. Then she thought of Mrs. Dalloway doubling and undoubling without a ripple. She thought of the plate-like thing in the ground and the way the world hesitated when she touched it. She thought of the government-looking men with their brochure smiles.

"Six," she finally responded.

"You're paying." A corner of his mouth moved or maybe it was a smile. Even just a tic hedging around one.

"Of course." He turned toward his Land Cruiser, then hesitated, just for a second, looking back at her. The sun caught his glasses, throwing a brief flare across the dust. Then he climbed in and drove off, leaving her standing in the heat with the hum of the sapphire still pulsing in her pocket steady, deliberate, and watching.

*
**

Later, in the Pub car park, the air carries the burn of petrol and evening dust. The horizon is gold, then blue, then something not quite definable, like as if it hasn't decided which version to render. Ella stands beside the back of her ute, sapphire in hand, stopwatch hanging around her neck like a charm. The barman, Mick, was equal parts friend and sceptic. He leans against the tray, chewing a stick of liquorice and eyeing her setup like it might explode at any moment.

"You really reckon that rocks got it in for you, eh?"

"Not in for me. More like in for physics." Ella said. Mick chuckles, his sun-creased face pulling tight.

"Have you been breathing too much of that generator exhaust again, love?"

"Just shut up and watch. I'm about to ruin your understanding of time." Ella insists as she sets the sapphire down on a stump, presses the stopwatch, and hums that same low tune. Something of a half-remembered Dreamtime melody, vibrating softly through the air.

The wind suddenly dies. So does the sound of

cicadas. Mick's chewing stops mid-bite. It literally stops. Ella glances up at Mick frozen solid, head tilted, eyes wide, liquorice halfway to his mouth.

"Right on cue." She whispers before circling him and snapping her fingers beside his ear. No reaction. His shirt ripples faintly in an unseen breeze that doesn't exist anymore. She lifts the sapphire again. The world felt delicate, like glass right before a fracture.

"If you're listening, whatever you are…this is your encore." She said dropping the sapphire into her hand. Just then, time resumes.

Mick blinks, then jumps back, dropping the liquorice.

"Bloody hell! You…you moved! You were…"

"Ahead of schedule, apparently." She laughed. Mick was visually shaken and confused.

"Hey, that's not funny! You were over there, then here! What the absolute…"

"See? Proof. Even the witness is confused." He glares at her, then at the rock, then at the sky.

"Maybe there's a gas leak. Or radiation. Or both."

"If it were radiation, you'd be glowing, and I'd finally have light out on my claim." Ella joked

The humour fades as both glance toward the distant ridge. For a moment, the light across the landscape flickers, the sunset rendering twice, two suns phasing out of sync. Mick whispers;

"Tell me that's not real."

"Oh, it's real alright. Just not ours." replied Ella. The soundscape warps, cicadas in chorus, then silence, then it doubled, slightly out of phase.

Mick steps back, crossing himself instinctively.

"You should call someone."

"I didn't have to. I was going to, but the universe answered first." Ella exclaimed.

She places the sapphire back in the pouch and looks up toward the pub, where its lights glitch twice before stabilising again.

At the New Royal, the heat squeezed inside the walls and sat at a table like a regular. The bar was nearly empty; too early for the miners who would come and salt the floor with their dusty footprints later. Mick polished a glass with a rag that never seemed to get anything cleaner.

Kael took a seat that gave him a good view of the door, window and the pub mirror with its gold-lettered pride in beer older than the patrons. Ella slid down onto a barstool opposite Kael. He set a notebook on the table but didn't open it.

'So, what do you think is happening?" Ella said abruptly before he could soften the edges.

Kael considered his answer like it might break if he dropped it wrong. 'I think this region sits on top of either a very old experiment or a very new technology. I think the plate-like things you found are part of some sort of network. I believe that some of the sapphires in this ground are... well...not exactly mineral. That they carry structures, information that can address this network."

'Like keys," Ella said, surprising herself with the word.

"Yes. Exactly like keys." He said as he blinked.

"And what about the people that find these keys?" She was careful not to touch the pouch at her throat.

'What is it that makes someone a...well...key-holder?" Ella continued.

'That I don't know." He hesitated.

'But some of you, some of us... seem to...resonate. You get these strange events clustered around you; you catch the corners of things that no one else sees. Maybe you're just more sensitive to patterns or maybe there's...something else."

"Something else...like what?" Ella pressed on for any answer that would help explain what was really going on. Kael didn't answer. Eyes down he turned his empty glass in his hands, the condensation leaving a perfect ring on the table.

"Have you noticed... repeats?" Ella frowned.

"Repeats?" He leaned forward, voice low.

"Conversations. Moments. Something happens and then it happens again, almost the same, with a minor difference. As if...someone...revised it."

The pub door creaked. Mick ambled over.

"You want another glass of wine, Ella? And something for your fancy friend?" Ella opened her mouth to answer.

"You want another glass of wine, Ella? And something for your fancy friend?" Mick said, same words, same lazy cadence. The second sentence tripped on a different syllable, like a bad edit.

Ella stared. Kael went very still.

"You all right?" Mick said. The third time. Not the same exactly, his eyebrow flicked a fraction higher, his rag dragged a different arc across the table, but the bones of the sentence were identical.

"Yeah," Ella said.

"We're fine for a bit, Mick." She heard her own voice trying to find a place to land.

"Two's good." Mick nodded and drifted back to the bar, the world recommitting to this version of itself.

"How long has this crazy stuff been happening?" Ella said. Kael breathed out.

"Here, a week. Other places there's been little hiccups. Then bigger ones. Things freeze. Duplicate. Anything in transit disappears from GPS for an hour and comes back like it took a different road."

"My neighbour doubled on my track this morning," Ella finally confessed. Just saying it made the room tilt.

"She couldn't have. There's no way. But she did." Kael studied her face as if the answer might be written in muscle under skin.

"You need to be careful who you tell this stuff too."

"You mean besides the man with the notebook and the institutional ID?"

"Especially him," he said, deadpan. He glanced at the mirror behind the bar. For an instant his reflection didn't match his posture, turning a fraction after he did, smile lagging. He flinched, a small honest motion, and then it was normal again.

Ella followed his gaze. Her own reflection stared back, tired around the eyes, hair escaping its clip. For a breath too long her reflection's hand stayed on the table while she reached up to push hair behind her ear. Then it caught up with a soft click she felt in her teeth.

"Do you hear it?" she asked.

"The clicks?"

"Sometimes," he said.

"Like…an audio track changing." He paused.

"Aunt May spoke to you." It wasn't a question. Ella set her jaw.

"She did."

"What did she say?" asked Kael

"That some stones are doors," Ella swallowed.

"That some people can hear when they open." Kael's expression didn't change into anything she could name.

"Then it's not just us," he murmured.

"They've known about all this for longer than we've been measuring."

"Who is the 'we' in that sentence, Kael?" Ella asked. He considered, then told the truth.

"People who ask questions for a living. Some are funded by universities. Some are funded by departments that don't put logos on brochures." He met her eyes.

"The men you saw today weren't from my team. So just be careful."

"Optional is still my favourite kind of no," Ella said, but it came out thinner than she'd liked.

The air in the pub shifted. A low buzz like a fridge motor coming on and never quite settling hummed under conversation. The ceiling fan stuttered, one blade stopped for a fraction of a rotation while the others continued, then all agreed to be a fan again.

"Do you ever…" Ella began, then stopped.

"What?" Kael prompted.

"Do you ever get the feeling…" She searched for a shape of words that wasn't a joke.

"That the world is a wireframe? And most days it's skinned and lit and textured and you don't notice what's underneath. And lately the skin's…thin. Like you can see the mesh." Kael stared at her for a long beat, the hum under the room balancing on the edge of louder.

"Yes," he said softly.

"Exactly like that." The hum cut off. Sound rushed in to fill the absence it left.

"Come with me," he said, decisively now.

"Not far. Just…there's something you should see. Tonight."

"Where?"

"Out past your claim. The plates. There's a cluster. We've been mapping them at night. Less noise."

"Noise," she repeated, and found the word fit several sizes of fear.

He stood, dropped cash on the table, and picked up the notebook he still hadn't opened.

"Bring the…lemon jam," he said, too fast for it to be a joke that made sense. Ella blinked. He realised what he'd said, and his mouth tightened.

"Sorry. My head's…ahh…editing."

"Yeah," Ella said. "Join the club."

They walked out into evening's last hard light.

The sky had the tinny pink of a song played through a cheap speaker. Dust lifted around their boots. An owl on the power line watched them go with a black eye that reflected two of each of them for a heartbeat, then decided on one.

Back at her caravan, Ella ducked inside for a torch and a second shirt. She paused with her hand on the drawer. The pouch hung against her chest, cool and insistent. If the world was a wireframe, this was a vertex, a point anchoring the whole. She lifted it from under her shirt and tucked it deeper, knotting the strings, then grabbed the torch.

The kerosene lamp hummed softly, painting everything in sepia. Outside, frogs sang like static trying to reassemble itself. The laptop screen glows faintly, casting her face in pale light.

Ella leans close to the camera, exhaustion lining her features but curiosity still burning beneath. She hits record.

"Test three, Rubyvale anomaly, timestamp unknown, since my clock's decided to play jazz with time signatures. The event's repeatable. The sapphire seems to create…let's call it a pause function. Everything stops except me, and apparently the battery life of this computer.

Witness report: Mick O'Connell. Currently denying reality and stress-eating liquorice at the pub. Hypothesis: either I've stumbled on quantum resonance between consciousness and crystal lattice structures…or I've finally lost the plot, and this is one very elaborate psychotic episode with props." She smirks, a glint of humour fighting through the fatigue.

"If anyone ever finds this recording…" Ella leans in closer,

"try not to make a documentary where I look like a lunatic, yeah?

For the record, I ran a full physical. Heart rate stable, blood oxygen fine. No evidence of hallucination…except for, you know…reality itself."

The lights flicker once. Her reflection on the laptop lags half a second behind.

"You're watching me, aren't you?" Ella murmurs and the screen stutters; her face duplicates for a single frame, overlapping itself before snapping back into sync.

"…Thought so." She said as she closed the lid

gently, whispering to the dark.

"Alright then, Bluey. Let's see who finds who first." She pockets the sapphire, blows out the lamp, and the screen fades to black.

*
**

Outside, lightning flickers soundlessly on the horizon, each flash slightly delayed, like the sky itself is buffering. Kael stood waiting by his Land Cruiser, engine off, listening. The air held that pressurised quiet Rubyvale got before a change. Somewhere, long away, thunder walked the ground polite as a visitor.

"Ready?" he said.

"As I'll ever be," Ella said.

They set off along the track toward the scrub where the earth rang hollow. Behind them the pub sign's light sputtered, went dark, and came back a different shade, different era, before choosing the colour it had always been. And above, just for a blink, the first star of the evening formed as a point on an invisible grid, snapped to its assigned place, and shone.

*
**

The night never quite settled after that. The air

carried a low vibration that wasn't wind and wasn't coming from a generator or wash plant, a hum just beneath hearing, like the sky itself was running diagnostics. Ella tried to sleep, but the caravan walls pulsed faintly with it, every screw and rivet shivering as if remembering another shape they'd once been.

Kael had driven off toward his camp hours ago, taillights blinking like red Morse code swallowed by dust. They'd barely spoken after what they'd seen, both pretending the silence was comfortable yet knowing it wasn't. When she'd turned to wave him off, the stars above the ridge had looked too evenly spaced, as if drawn by hand.

Inside the van, she lay on her back, staring at the ceiling cracks. Somewhere outside, a curlew screamed; it was the kind of sound that made locals mutter about death or change, depending on who was listening. Ella turned on her side, clutching the pouch to her chest. The sapphire's cool weight felt steady against her skin, but now and then it seemed to pulse once, faintly, in time with her heartbeat.

By the time she drifted into shallow sleep, the hum had faded, leaving only the desert's soft static and the occasional cough of 12–volt fan.

Then…just before dawn…came another sound.

Low, distant, deliberate…Engines.

01010100 01101000 01100101 00100000 01000011
01110010 01111001 01110011 01110100 01100001
01101100 00100000 01000011 01101111 01100100
01100101

"The closer we look at matter,
the more it behaves like memory."

-Dr. Kael Nathan, Field Notes

CHAPTER FIVE
GOVERNMENT MOVES IN

The convoy came at dawn. Ella was already outside, boots laced, kettle hissing on the gas burner when the first engine rumbled down the track. She froze, kettle forgotten, as three dark-green trucks rolled into Rubyvale like they owned it. Not miners' utes. Not tourists' campers; these had antennae sprouting from their roofs, windows dark as obsidian…number plates that didn't belong to Queensland.

Old Stan wandered out in his dressing gown, still looking half-asleep, mug of tea in hand, and squinted at the convoy.

"Well," he called out, voice echoing down the empty track,

"looks like someone's finally remembered we exist. Took 'em long enough… Usually you've got to catch fire or flood before Canberra remembers this place is even on the map, even then we are forgotten."

The trucks slowed down, doors opening in sequence. Men and women in desert-camouflage uniforms stepped out, their boots striking dust that hadn't seen polish in decades. They had rifles slung openly over their shoulders, scanning the scrub like it might bite. Stan snorted into his tea.

"Bloody Canberra," he muttered.

"Last time they came this far west was in '89, when they promised to seal the road to Anakie and boost regional prosperity." He took a sip.

"The only thing they sealed was their own bloody fuel allowance and the only thing they boosted was the motel profits." He'd never forgiven them for that, or for what came a few years later when the Department of Minerals decided to 'rationalise' the diggings. They'd sent in men with clipboards, no hats, to shut down half the claims under some policy buzzword no one could pronounce, and left families packing up their dreams in old Landcruisers. Stan had watched his neighbours leave one by one until he was one of the few left, stubborn as the granite.

"They took my brother's lease, too," he said to no one in particular, just the dust.

"Promised compensation. We're still waiting on the bloody cheque."

He raised his mug toward the soldiers in a mock salute.

"Welcome back, useless bloody government. Don't go straining yourselves now." Ella watched him with a faint smile tugging at the corner of her mouth. There was something oddly reassuring about Old Stan and his morning ritual of defiance. He'd become part of the landscape, a landmark in flannel and faded slippers. To the newcomers, he was just another cranky old miner with too much sun and not enough sense, but to the Gemfields regulars, Stan was a story that still walked around.

He'd been here longer than the rust on the drums, longer than most of the claims themselves...a living reminder of what stubbornness looked like when it grew callouses and drank its tea strong and black. The younger fossickers called him the Postmaster General or PM for short, only because he had opinions to deliver to anyone who'd listen.

Ella had grown up hearing his name in half the local stories, sometimes as a hero, sometimes as the cautionary ending to it. He'd once chained himself to a grader to stop it flattening a working small-scale claim, and another time he'd taken a council official's ute keys hostage for safekeeping until they agreed to fix the water pump that pumped water from the standpipe. Yet somehow, he'd always walked away with a grin and a beer.

She'd never been sure if it was courage, madness, or just the kind of luck that came from outstaring the sun. But watching him now, squinting at the uniformed strangers on his dirt, Ella felt a flicker of both pride and worry. Stan was the Gemfields in human form, half fossil and half rebellion, and she had a feeling that whatever lay in the future, men like him were about to go extinct all over again.

One of the soldiers who was younger than the dust and fresh from somewhere with air-conditioning, raised a clipboard and squinted at the papers clipped to it.

'Stanley Ridgeway?' he called out, reading from the list.

'Mine Claim holder of 998751?'

Stan straightened just slightly, the way you do when someone uses your full name like an accusation.

'Depends...who's asking,' he said. The soldier hesitated, glancing at his commanding officer before continuing. 'Your claim falls within the restricted survey perimeter. You'll need to cease all operations and leave your claim immediately.' Stan barked a short laugh.

'Operations? Mate, the only operation I'm running is trying to get my kettle to boil before the world ends. Tell Canberra she's safe.' He took a long sip from his mug, but Ella noticed the tremor in his fingers. It wasn't fear. Not exactly. It was something older. The kind of dread that comes from knowing the pattern's repeating, and this time it might not stop with paperwork.

The officer made a note on her tablet.

'He's on the register,' she said quietly to the man beside her.

"Mark him down as a high-probability contact." Ella's stomach twisted. She didn't know what that meant, but she didn't like the sound of it. Out here in the Gemfields, being noticed by a government authority was *never* a good thing.

Stan muttered under his breath, just loud enough for her to hear.

"First they write your name down," he said, eyes fixed on the soldier's tablet.

"Then they write your history for you."

A tall, staunch-looking woman in mirrored sunglasses spoke, her voice amplified by the silence.

"This area is now restricted under federal law for the purpose of a surveying geological instability. All authority to mine on claims within this area has been suspended until further notice. Please remain on your claim until instructed otherwise. I repeat, this area is now restricted under federal law, and all mining is to be suspended immediately, please remain on your claims." Ella felt her gut twist. Geological instability was one of those phrases bureaucrats loved. Big enough to sound official, vague enough to cover anything. It could mean sinkholes, tremors, landslides…or whatever the hell they wanted it to mean. Out here, it usually translated to we're taking over, and don't bother asking questions. But the weight of her pouch against her chest told her exactly what geological instability was cover for.

The stone inside felt heavier than it should, as if aware of the lie hanging in the Rubyvale air. She didn't need a press release to know what they were really after out here, whatever it was humming beneath the dirt had finally made itself impossible to ignore.

Kael appeared at her shoulder, breath uneven from jogging up from his camp. A fine layer of red dust turned the sweat on his skin into mud. He didn't look surprised, and for Ella, that was worse than panic. Surprise meant shock, which meant you hadn't planned for this. Whereas calm meant you had.

"They're here already," he whispered, eyes tracking the convoy like he'd been waiting for it. Stan barked a laugh, the sound rough as gravel.

"Instability, my arse. That's bloody Canberra talk for 'we're taking your dirt.'" He raised his mug in a mock toast.

"Cheers, you pompous bastards." The tall woman in mirrored sunglasses flicked her gaze toward him but didn't bother replying. She didn't have to, the reflection already showed him disappearing behind his own dust.

All around her, soldiers fanned out across the fields with practiced precision, unspooling yellow cordon tape and hammering metal stakes into the ground that had seen more shovels than sunlight. They worked fast and efficient, like they were claiming a crime scene instead of a small town.

The old vintage fences were cut without asking. A hand-painted sign reading 'Mine Claim - Keep Out' was flattened coldly under a steel-capped military boot. One of the neighbour's dogs barked from behind a fence until eventually one of the soldiers shouted at it and the dog went quiet. The red dirt seemed to swallow every sound except the wind and the soft click of tape being pulled tighter.

Ella's fingers found the sapphire through the fabric of her shirt. Cold. Steady. Its edges pressed against her skin like a heartbeat out-of-sync. She imagined, absurdly, that it was watching them back, recording every movement, every word. The soldiers scanned the ground with their machines, but she had the feeling the stone was scanning them back.

By midday, Rubyvale felt like a town under siege. The pub shut its doors, though Mick stayed inside polishing glasses no one would drink from. Diggers stood at fences, arms folded, staring at men with clipboards who measured ground like it belonged to them. The air had that unnatural quiet, the kind that happens when everyone's pretending not to stare.

One of the old diggers, John, lit a cigarette at his gate.

'So, what's the drill, love?" he asked one of the more serious looking soldiers.

"You lot gonna shoot us if we dig too hard?" The soldier didn't reply. John smirked.

"Yeah, didn't think so. Ya wouldn't even find your bullets again once they hit this dirt."

Ella and Kael sat in the shade of her caravan, keeping low. He scribbled diagrams in his notebook: lines, lattices, grids. His diagrams looked a lot like the ones in her dream but tidier.

"They've been tracking the anomalies," he said.

"Glitches, repeats, duplications. They've found enough data points, and they've triangulated here."

'So, you knew they'd come," Ella quickly accused.

"I suspected," Kael said, his pencil stopped on the page.

"But not this fast."

A loud crack rang out. For one panicked second Ella thought it was gunfire, after all, it was the Gemfields, where tempers ran as hot as the engines and most disputes were settled with shouting, swearing, or the occasional warning shot into the dust. But it was only old Tommy from Reward, throwing a hammer onto the ground, shouting about his second claim. Two soldiers had wrestled him back while a third one sealed off his wash plant.

"They'll take everything," Ella said, voice low.

"I'm sure they'll try," Kael murmured.

"You say that like you've seen this sort of thing before." Ella said curiously and Kael hesitated.

"I have, yes. Just never in daylight, not like this."

The late afternoon brought a different breed of threat. Not soldiers this time, but men in white shirts and broad-brimmed hats, the kind of clean you could only get from an office. They carried clipboards, GPS scanners that beeped like confused birds, and expressions that said we're here to help while their boots said we've never been outside before.

They moved through camp with a kind of polite predation, asking for signatures they were never going to get, pointing out boundaries that had already been lived in for decades.

Old Stan leaned against his fence, cigarette dangling from his mouth, and watched one of them measure his claim with the precision of a man timing toast.

"You lot even know what you're looking for, or what?" he called.

One of the men looked up and smiled the way people do when they've already decided you're irrelevant.

"Unregistered mineral anomalies, sir."

Stan spat into the dirt.

"Yeah, mate. Well, out here we call that luck."

The man wrote something on his clipboard, nodded like that meant he'd won the exchange, and walked away. Stan watched him go, muttering,

"Bloody hell, look at that, will Ya? They've got paperwork for hope now."

Meanwhile, in town, a drone hovered low over Keilambete Road, its rotors whining like a mosquito that refused to die. The red camera light blinked in steady rhythm, sweeping across the corrugated rooftops, the old cafe, the single blinking streetlamp that hadn't worked properly since 2003. Dust lifted in lazy spirals beneath it, as if even the air was tired of being watched.

A soldier stood by the post office, holding some sort of handheld sensor that looked half-science, half-guesswork. Every time he turned west, toward Goanna Flats Road, the device let out a sharp electronic chirp.

"I'm picking up fluctuations," he said, either to himself or into a 2-way that no one else could hear. Mick, watching from the pub window with a schooner half-poured, couldn't be sure.

"That's just a heat shimmer, mate," Mick called out, leaning against the flyscreen.

"Or maybe it's a hangover shimmer. Hard to tell the difference round here."

The soldier didn't answer. He crouched, pulled a small silver probe from his vest pocket, and dropped it into the dirt. It sank straight down without resistance, like the ground had been waiting to swallow it.

"Very porous substructure," he reported into his headset.

"That," Mick said from across the street,

"it's called a hole, mate. You'll find plenty of 'em round here." He took a long sip from his mug, eyes never leaving the soldier.

"You want my professional opinion, I'd say it's one of the better holes we've got, classic depth, fine local texture, near-mint condition."

A few of the onlookers chuckled. Mick wasn't done.

"Got another one of those fancy gadgets to tell you our water's wet too? Or maybe you've got an app for that?" The soldier ignored him, which only encouraged the laughter.

The soldiers' eyes narrowed as he studied his readout. The numbers jittered, skipping from positive to negative like they couldn't decide what world they belonged to. One second the screen flashed metallic signatures: iron, nickel, traces of copper, then suddenly organic, almost biological. He tapped the side of the sensor and frowned. His radio crackled back to life, but the sound that came through wasn't the normal static sound. Instead, two voices spoke at once, same words, same tone, half a second out of sync.

He pulled his earpiece out. The sound continued anyway, faint but deliberate, bleeding into the air like something broadcast through the dirt itself. Beneath the hum of the drone, Mick swore he heard it too, it was a woman's voice humming, soft and steady, somewhere under the noise floor.

Mick looked up from his mug.

"You get that on your fancy scanner, did ya?" The soldier said nothing. But his hand trembled slightly as he marked the coordinates on his map, and for the first time that day, he looked afraid.

The afternoon dragged toward dusk, heat still clinging to the air like a held breath. The soldiers had finished pegging their markers and were packing up, but the feeling of being watched hadn't left. Even the magpies had gone quiet. Mick leaned against the pub's veranda rail, watching one of the soldiers take soil readings by the old water tank.

"You ever notice," he said to Ella, who'd wandered up beside him, "how these government types always act like they're on the moon instead of just west of Emerald?" She didn't answer. The air felt thick and charged just how the air feels just before a summer storm, only the sky was perfectly clear. One of the handheld scanners on the bonnet of a truck began to beep in uneven pulses.

"Interference," the woman who appeared to be in charge said curtly

"Check frequency drift."

"Copy," came a reply. The soldier with the probe frowned at his device.

"It's reading null, then full saturation then null again. It looks like the signal's folding in on itself."

"Could be iron in the soil," his partner offered, though her voice lacked conviction.

"Yeah," Mick yelled,

"and I'm the bloody Tooth Fairy."

Ella squinted toward the horizon. Heat shimmered off the dirt, but beneath it something else flickered. The light bent, just slightly, as if the ground had inhaled. Then it stilled. When she blinked, it was gone.

A radio crackled nearby with double-talk. Two identical voices speaking the same words a half-beat apart.

"Repeat, this is Unit Six ... six ...confirm ... firm..."

The commanding officer slapped her earpiece.

"Cut the cross-feed."

"Already did, ma'am," said the tech.

"The duplication isn't on our channel."

Ella glanced at Mick, who looked pale now under the veranda lights. The radio chatter died off one channel at a time, leaving only the whisper of wind and the soft ticking of cooling metal. The soldiers gathered their equipment in uneasy silence, folding up their tripods like men packing away a crime scene they didn't understand.

The convoy's engines rumbled to life and one by one the trucks turned toward the main road, headlights cutting cones of white through the haze. Dust rolled through the dying light like smoke, clinging to the fences and the gum leaves, making the whole town look half-erased. Mick stood at the edge of the veranda, mug in hand.

"You ever seen government clear out that fast?" he asked, confused.

Ella shook her head.

"No. Usually they stay long enough to name something after themselves." He gave a grim laugh.

"Guess they didn't like what their toys found."

As the last truck crawled up the rise, Ella caught it, just a flicker, a pulse of light deep in the scrub beyond the flats. It was faint and blue almost like the reflection of lightning that never quite happened. It blinked once, twice, then went still, leaving an afterimage in her vision that wouldn't fade.

"See that?" she murmured. Mick frowned, shielding his eyes.

"Nah. Just dusk playing tricks on Ya, Girl." But Ella

knew dusk didn't hum like that. The sound started low, so low she thought it was in her head. A tremor more than a tone that was vibrating through both her boots and the boards beneath them. She turned toward the window that led out to the darkening horizon.

That night, back at her claim, the desert hummed. A sound too low to be wind, too steady to be machines. Lights carved through the scrub, harsh white beams sweeping back and forth like searchlights, cutting the night into moving pieces. Every few seconds, one would catch on the tin of a roof or a rusted miner's ute, flashing like distant lightning that never quite arrived.

At some point, the air thickened and Ella could taste a metallic tang on her tongue. Ella sat at the small table inside her caravan, the one held together by a zip tie and faith, trying to ignore the way her mug rattled on the surface. The lightbulb overhead buzzed in sympathy, flickering to an unseen rhythm. Outside, the night was too still. No wind, no insects, just the hum, steady as a heartbeat, coming from everywhere and nowhere. It threaded through the gravel and the air, through the bones of the caravan and the soles of her feet. Her pouch sat heavy against her chest, and she found herself gripping it tight, as if the stone inside might leap out.

Out across the ridge, faint lights swept like restless

ghosts. Harsh, artificial, cutting the landscape into moving strips. She could hear the low murmur of soldiers' radios somewhere in the dark. A woman's voice, sharp and uncertain:

"Unit Three, report visual...?"

"-copy-copy-copy-"

The words echoed three times, layered, as if the signal itself had learned to mimic.

*
**

Ella crept down from the caravan steps, barefoot now. The dust was cool and damp under her feet, the way it gets just before the dew sets. When she reached the edge of her claim line, she froze.

Out there, near the flat where the soldiers had been scanning earlier, the ground glowed. A dull sapphire-blue pulse, faint but rhythmic, like a vein beneath skin. A few soldiers stood around it, their outlines black against the eerie light. She couldn't hear their words, only the sound of one man's breath catching. Then suddenly, motion as one of them bent to touch the glow. The pulse flared a deep surge of colour that turned the dust silver, and the soldier jerked upright, rifle slipping from his hands.

For a second, there were two of him, perfect doubles. Two silhouettes screaming in unison, sound warped and split like a skipping record. Then one image snapped out of existence, leaving only dust where the duplicate had stood. Ella clapped a hand over her mouth, backing away until her spine hit the datum post. The other soldiers pulled him back and shouting words that didn't carry far enough for her to hear.

Something shifted behind her. Kael's voice, quiet and careful:

"They don't know what they're holding." Ella turned, startled. He stood half in shadow, his face ghost-pale in the reflected blue.

"Neither do we," she whispered.

Kael's eyes flicked toward her chest, to the pouch under her shirt, the stone pressing cool against her skin.

"You're wrong El," he said softly.

"Yours talks back."

*
**

Later that night, by the now dying campfire, Kael spoke quietly.

"You ever think that we might be the real intruders here?" Ella smirked, poking at the coals with a stick.

"Speak for yourself, city boy. I was here first." She laughed, but the sound came out softer than she meant it to. He looked at her, long and thoughtfully.

"Not first, Ella. Just next."

The wind shifted, carrying the scent of burnt timber and rain that never came. The sand made a faint, crystalline sound, like static whispering secrets between the grains. Somewhere far below the earth, the hum kept humming.

For a while, neither of them spoke. The firelight flickered against their faces, his calm and analytical, hers tired and wary. Two people lit by a glow that felt older than either of them. Kael broke the silence.

"You know, I used to think places like this didn't exist anymore. The kind of towns that live on stubbornness alone."

'Stubbornness and beer," Ella said.

'Don't forget the essentials." He smiled, but it didn't quite reach his eyes.

"You make jokes when you're scared."

"Yeah? And you analyse when you should shut up," she said, smiling back at him. That comment had earned her an actual laugh, short and genuine as if he hadn't done it in a long time. They fell quiet again, the sound of the fire filling the gaps. Ella glanced at him.

"You really believe all that?" she asked.

"About arrays, interfaces, whatever the hell you called them?" Kael's gaze didn't move from the flames.

'Belief isn't the right word. It's more like…recognition. The world's trying to tell us something, and most people stopped listening to a long time ago." Ella tilted her head.

"And you think I'm supposed to listen?"

"I think you already are," he said simply.

The words landed between them, heavier than the night. For a long moment, she couldn't tell if the warmth rising in her chest was from the fire or from something else, she hadn't felt in a long time, something that scared her more than the hum ever could.

A faint shimmer ran through the coals. A quick blue spark, gone before either could speak. The hum deepened, soft but present, curling beneath their voices like a secret heartbeat.

Kael leaned back, eyes reflecting the last of the flames.

"If you start hearing music in the stones," he said,

"promise me you'll tell me first."

Ella snorted.

"What makes you think I'd tell you anything?"

"Because," he said, looking at her now,

"You already did." The fire cracked, a single ember flaring into the night before fading into black. Somewhere far below, the earth exhaled.

01100110 01101100 01101111 01110111 00100000
01101111 01100110 00100000 01101100 01101001
01100111 01101000 01110100

CHAPTER SIX
THE INSIDER'S WARNING

Rubyvale slept uneasy under the slow sweep of the government floodlights. Ella couldn't sleep at all. Every time she shut her eyes, the image replayed: the soldier duplicating, screaming in stereo, then snapping back into one. Not a glitch, not a hallucination. She knew what she saw. And worse, she knew what it meant.

At midnight she gave up. Quietly, she slipped into her boots, careful not to wake anyone next-door. The air was too still, yet highly charged. Even the insects seemed to be holding their breath. She just needed some space. Some fresh air. A little distance from the walls and the quiet, suffocating sense that something in the camp had changed since the soldier split and screamed in stereo. She hadn't told anyone. How could she? They'd think she was losing it, or worse… they may be right.

She didn't turn on her torch; she didn't need to as her feet knew the dirt paths by instinct. Past the old abandoned mine shaft, through the spinifex that snagged her jeans like little hands. Ella was not entirely sure where she was going; she just knew she needed space. Anything to stop the echo of that scream in her skull.

She crossed the dry creek bed and paused at the broken fencepost marking the edge of the old, designated fossicking area. The government claimed it was all off-limits now, but everyone still came here, the locals, fossickers and memory-drunk tourists. The earth was littered with forgotten things. Tools, bottles, and dreams. She sat down on an old timber sleeper half-sunken into the red dust. And for a while, she just stared off into the dark sky and tried to think of nothing. Harsh and still. No shimmer, no twinkle. They seemed slightly wrong. Too perfect, as if the sky didn't breathe anymore.

She rubbed her arms. The night had cooled sharply, but that wasn't why she was cold. She turned, drawn by instinct, and stared into the bush behind her.

Nothing.

But Ella felt something was watching. She just knew it. She stood up slowly and began to walk with a pace a little faster than the one she had used to get there. Her legs carried her downhill, half-running before she realised where she was headed: the dam.

The dam was just a shallow, silty hollow these days, but it still held water from the last rains. A moon hung low over it, and the surface reflected just enough light to cast shadows across its banks. And there... by the edge...was Kael.

Ella stopped.

He was crouched down, skipping stones. Alone. Shirt sleeves rolled to the elbows, torch off, like her. Like maybe he couldn't sleep either.

"Couldn't stay inside?" he asked without turning.

"Nope," she said.

"Too much strangeness to settle down."

"Too many people." He looked up and grinned faintly.

She walked down to join him, careful not to slip on the slope. Sat a few feet away. He offered her a flat stone, already chosen. She tossed it. Three skips.

"Nice," he said. They sat like that for a while, just two lonely figures by a tired dam, flicking ripples into silence. Eventually, she asked,

"Do you think we're really alone out here?" Kael didn't answer right away. He picked up another stone, then said,

"In what way?" Ella paused.

"I don't know, in any way, I guess." Kael tossed the stone. It plunked and then sank.

"No," he said softly. His simple response was enough for Ella.

Eventually, Kael stood.

"I should head back before the patrols get twitchy," he said, brushing off his jeans. Ella nodded, though she didn't move.

"You go ahead." He hesitated.

"You sure? Are you going to be okay out here alone?"

"Yeah, of course," she said.

"Just need a minute."

Kael gave her a slow look, unreadable in the half-light, then turned and crunched off through the gravel. His footsteps faded quickly, swallowed by distance and dust.

Ella sat a little longer, watching the moon ripple in the muddy water. For a moment, she imagined diving into its water, just letting the cold, red earth swallow her whole. A strange longing flickered through her: what would it feel like to disappear entirely?

She shook the thought loose and decided it was time to head back. As she climbed the embankment, her boots left fresh prints in the soft red dirt. She followed them for a while without thinking. The walk was quiet again. The cicadas had returned, their buzz low and steady now, like background static. But then...something strange.

At a bend near the edge of the old quartz flats, she saw a second set of prints beside her own. Not Kael's. They looked like hers. Same tread. Same depth. Same stride. But she hadn't come this way before. Ella stopped dead. Her heart gave a single hard thud.

She turned slowly, following the phantom trail with

her eyes. The duplicate prints veered off into the bush to the east, toward the sealed shaft known as *Whistler's Drop*. A place the older timers warned people to stay away from. Gran used to say it echoed back wrong when you shouted.

She crouched, pressed her fingers to one of the prints. They seemed still warm. She stood. Something was moving in parallel to her. Same direction. Same steps. Same shape. The humming started again. It was very low like it was coming from beneath the crust of the earth.

She heard it behind her then a whisper of movement, like dry leaves scraping glass. Her name… spoken without voice.

"Ella." She spun around. But the bush behind her was empty. The hum didn't stop, and her footprints kept going.

Above her, the stars glared down, hard and clear. It appeared like a rendered sky with the brightness turned up. The Milky Way shimmered in place yet not a single star twitched. The air was taut and stretched thin between things. Somewhere in the distance, a bird of some kind shrieked, then silence. Ella froze. The cicadas that were ever-present since dusk had stopped all at once. Not faded but completely stopped. As if a music conductor had cut the sound with his baton.

She crouched low. The hairs on her arms stood up.

The ground felt like it was humming faintly, a deep frequency that was more felt than heard. Ella started to feel a pressure build behind her eyes, like she'd climbed too high in too little time. Her breath came faster, shallow. Something was wrong. Not just military-wrong. Reality-wrong. The kind of wrong that doesn't leave footprints.

And then...footsteps. They certainly were not hers and they were not human. They didn't crunch like boots, instead they whispered like static, dragging across gravel in soft, scraping rhythms. Left. Right. Left. Then silence. Then again, closer.

Ella ducked behind a mulga tree, heart slamming hard against her chest. She reached instinctively for the pocketknife in her jacket, completely useless, but it was something. A cold breeze swept through the scrub. No scent. No sound. Something was close.

And then, ahead just past the rise of the hill leading up to the flat she liked to watch the sunset from, a silhouette somewhat shimmered into appearance. Not walking...glitching forward in a weird non-human-like motion. She stood up slowly, pressing her back to the tree trunk and being careful not to move.

The shimmer paused for a moment, pulsing faintly like heat haze only it wasn't heat. It was after midnight, the temperature had dropped sharply, and the wind had picked up. The shimmer slowly became a shape. A figure, but not quite. Too tall, limbs slightly out of proportion. Its head tilted, like it was listening to something Ella couldn't hear. Or someone she couldn't see. She squinted, trying not to blink. Her breath clouded, misting in the cold air, which seemed to grow colder.

The figure stepped forward. It didn't walk in a human-like way; it slid. Its body flickered with interference, like a corrupted computer file trying to hold its form. Limbs warped, outlines lagged behind movement, like an animation buffering on a failing signal. One shoulder jerked, then repeated. A hand re-formed in the wrong position before correcting itself. It wasn't broken; it looked like a computer game that was decoding.

Ella felt a memory surface. Not a thought but a return. As if something dormant in her was being activated by proximity. However, it was as if she wasn't the one remembering - it was the one remembering her.

Her grandmother's voice came back in a flash. It was so vivid, she could almost smell the smoke of burnt eucalyptus and whiskey on the old woman's breath. They had been camped near Snake Hollow, not far from the old diggings that were now fenced off by the government. Gran always said that place hummed differently. "I never really knew what she meant."

"The Gemfields don't forget, my girl," Gran had whispered one night, poking at the coals. "Not like people do. They hold what's dropped. Even time. Even names."

"Deep below, there's a place the maps don't show, and that's where the shadows go to sleep. They take your shape when the surface gets too noisy. They move like they are dreams, but they aren't. They're the echoes from before the mines, from before even the stones themselves. They are not spirits nor ghosts...Something older, laced into the code of the earth." she'd say occasionally.

Ella hadn't understood at the time. She thought it was a ghost story. It had always scared her. She'd believed it was just a story to stop children wandering too far. But Gran had always been strange. She was wired into things that others dismissed and claimed her bloodline was part dreamer, part something that still remembered the time before mining licenses and survey maps.

"They want the stories in your skin, not the sapphires in your pocket," Gran had said once.

"Every gem is a recording. You touch one wrong, and you may let something out, or worse, wake something up." And now...here it was.

The figure shimmered again, and this time, its form

clicked into a new shape. Ella's shape. Her exact stance. Her jacket. Her hair pulled back the same way. Even the old leather pendant around her neck, the one with the faded engraving of The Cracked Eye like a glyph from the dream maps Gran once drew on butcher's paper and buried in tin boxes across the fields.

The face that looked back at her was hers, but subtly unnervingly wrong. The left eye blinked half a second too late. The breath didn't fog in the air. And its hands...its hands were turning inward, as if unfolding into keys.

The figure mouthed her name.

"Ella." No sound. Just the shape of the word on lips that weren't quite real. The ground beneath her boots thrummed in response as if the name had activated something below. Not a voice, but maybe a signal, waiting for her.

She knew, then, without logic, that this thing had been waiting here, in one of those buried vaults that Gran had spoken of in feverish tones before the dementia took her. Not because of who she was. But because of what she carried. A bloodline, a memory, a pattern or a frequency encoded into her DNA like a forgotten passcode.

And now...something had logged in uninvited.

Suddenly Ella heard her own voice saying something she never expected.

"We're not from here, are we?" She clamped her jaw shut.

"Don't think too loud," she thought to herself.

The figure turned its head, slowly and unnaturally as if it heard her and for a moment, its face stabilised. It was hers. But wrong. Not a reflection, not a twin, more like an echo. Eyes hollow, mouth flickering in and out of sync. It mouthed something like

"Ella." But with no sound. Just the shape of the word, perfectly timed with the pulsing hum from beneath the ground. She staggered back, breath catching, and the illusion broke. The figure dissolved into a storm of noise and distortion, like a screen losing signal. It vanished before she could scream.

The cicadas resumed, as if someone hit play. But the hum didn't stop. It had only gotten louder. The air was taut, as if stretched thin between things that wanted to happen. Cicadas faltered again. A whisper came from the dark.

"You shouldn't leave it alone." Ella spun, hand instinctively on the pouch.

A dark figure stepped from the mulga shadows. Tall, wiry, clothes dust-stained, but its outline flickered, not with torchlight but with something wrong. For a second, two of him overlapped. The same face, one looking a fraction to the left, one to the right, before collapsing into one again.

The figure raised empty hands.

"Don't run. You've seen enough to know I'm not lying."

"Who the hell are you?" Ella demanded.

"A remnant," he said. His voice carried an echo, as if one syllable lagged the next.

"Call me the Insider, if names help."

"What do you want?" He tilted his head.

"To warn you. They'll come for your stone. The ones with guns, the one with the notebook, even the elders. But none of them can use it. Only you."

Ella's stomach dropped.

"Why me?" The Insider's smile was weary, almost kind.

"Because you're not...entirely theirs. Half of you is... written...Code...You've felt it, haven't you? The missteps. The déjà vu too sharp. The world...catching up to you."

Her throat went dry.

"That's heatstroke. Bad dreams."

"Is it?" He stepped closer; for a moment his outline blurred again, two frames misaligned.

"You're a bridge Ella. Human enough to move among them. Written enough to touch the network. That's why the stone woke in your hand."

'Stop.' Her voice cracked.

'I'm not...Whatever you think!'

'You are,' he said gently.

'And the choice will be yours, much sooner than you want.'

From the track at the bottom of the hill, a searchlight swung, and soldiers' voices carried sharp orders. The figure glanced toward them, then back to her.

'They'll rewrite you if they can. Better you write yourself first.' He reached out, fingers almost touching her arm, then froze. His face twisted, as though resisting some invisible grip. His outline split violently into three, staggered images stuttering around him.

'Time's thin,' he gasped.

'Remember the grid. Remember the song.' And with a sharp crack, he vanished like a skipped frame edited from a reel.

Ella stumbled back, heart thundering, staring at empty scrub. The cicadas resumed, loud and oblivious. The sapphire against her chest burned cold. Behind her, Kael's voice came low and urgent.

'Who were you talking to?' She spun. He stood ten paces back, torch off, face pale.

'You followed me?' she demanded.

'You were shouting,' Kael said. His eyes darted to

the dark scrub around them, then back to her.

"There was no one here." Ella clutched the pouch, fingers white.

"There was." Kael shook his head.

"You're rattled. The stress…"

"No." Her voice was as hard as steel.

"He said I'm part of this, not just a witness." Kael's mouth tightened, but he didn't deny it.

Somewhere beyond the ridge, Aunt May's chant rose again. Low, rhythmic, patient as the earth. And for a flicker of a second, Ella thought she saw the grid overlay the night sky, stars pinned to invisible intersections. Somewhere, deeper than stone, a memory uncoiled. And something old enough to remember her before she was born had just begun to wake. She pressed the pouch hard against her chest. For the first time, she wasn't sure if she was holding the stone or if the stone was holding her.

The silence that followed wasn't empty, it was listening. The kind that settled after a question is asked but not yet answered. Ella turned slowly, scanning the darkness for any movement, but what scared her wasn't what she might see, it was what might see her. The pouch pulsed once, slow and deliberate, and in that moment, she knew something had marked her. Not as an intruder. Not even as a threat. But as a key. Something that was waiting not to be found, but instead to be unlocked.

111

CHAPTER SEVEN
THE CRYSTALS CONNECT

The sun hit its peak like a branding iron, turning the metal of the survey tower into a vertical oven. Ella wiped the sweat from her brow with the back of her hand and squinted up at the top bracket.

'Should've brought the long wrench," she said.

"Did bring the long wrench," Kael said from below, handing it up to her without looking. He was in the shade of the ute with a tablet on his knees, monitoring voltage readouts like a man trying to reason with ghosts. She took the wrench and gave the panel frame a final tighten. The whole thing groaned back into alignment.

"There," she said.

"Realigned and didn't even get electrocuted."

Kael stood up and shaded his eyes.

"We'll test the charge flow in five."

Ella climbed down, her boots hitting the red dirt with a thud.

"This one's been glitching since Monday," he said.

"You think it's the dust?"

Ella gave him a look.

"Out here? Almost always the dust."

He half-smiled, but he didn't quite crack one.

'It's more than that. Look at this…" *Kael* turned the tablet toward her.

The screen showed a visual map of energy flow between towers, an overlay of pulsing lines. One node, the one that represented this tower, was flaring erratically, like a firework caught mid-fizzle.

'See that pattern?" he asked. "Almost rhythmic."

Ella crossed her arms.

'Or just old hardware and sunstroke."

Kael's brow creased.

'I'm telling you Ella, something's cycling through these towers. A signal loop. It's faint, but it's consistent." He said as he picked up her canteen and took a swig.

'You mean the government's little underground experiment is bleeding out into the solar grid?" Ella replied with sarcasm. He hesitated.

'Maybe, or maybe there's more to this Gemfields terrain than they understand."

Ella cocked her head.

'You really believe that don't you? That you can measure the unknown into submission. Turn a mystery into data points."

Kael didn't rise to the bait. He just looked at her, calmly and said,

"And you really believe intuition trumps evidence."

'I believe the evidence gets edited." Ella shrugged.

They both stood in silence, sun baking the top of their heads as the weight of unsaid things began stacking between them.

Snapping them back into the moment, the radio on Kael's hip crackled to life.

'Station Five to Base. Copy. Picking up cross-frequency noise on patrol loop. Intermittent burst, low Hz. Not weather-related. Might be...some kind of...feedback. Requesting scan.'

Kael grabbed it.

'Base here. Confirming interference?'

'Confirmed,' came the voice again, fuzzy now.

'It's...weird. Like it's under the floor.' A static pop ended the message.

Kael looked at Ella. She raised an eyebrow.

'Still just faulty wiring?' She asked, but he didn't answer.

They returned to camp by late afternoon. The heat had settled into that strange, weightless lull that only happens in the hour before dusk when the land holds its breath. Aunt May sat on the shaded side of the billy-boulder hut, peeling mandarins with her eyes half-closed. Her long skirt brushed the wooden planks like soft static. She wasn't watching them, but her head tilted slightly when they approached. Ella flopped onto the bottom

115

stair.

"Towers fixed. Maybe."

"Panel's holding," Kael added, dropping the toolkit beside her but Aunt May gave no sign of listening. But then she began to hum. Softly, tunelessly at first then it shaped itself into something structured that had a familiar melody. Ella frowned. The song drifted around them, fragile as smoke. Not English. Not language at all yet it tugged at the edges of a memory, as if she'd heard it before. Perhaps as a child, in a fever or maybe even a dream.

"Down where the sapphires dream alone...

Under root and dust and bone...

Mark the light but walk it slow...

It shows you what you're meant to know-"

Aunt May peeled the last mandarin, popping a segment into her mouth without pause in the melody. Ella glanced at Kael.

"You hearing this?"

He nodded, slowly.

"She's been humming that for days. I thought it was just...I don't know. An old miner's lullaby or something?" But the way the notes fell, the subtle repetition, the rhythmic rise and fall, it wasn't just a tune. It was a pattern. There was something about it made the sapphire in Ella's pouch press a little warmer against her chest.

The sky was sliding into copper and ash by the time Ella wandered past the last fencepost, following the sloping path that led toward the edge of the claims. She wasn't sure why her feet had carried her all the way out here, maybe to walk off the heat still clinging to her skin, maybe to escape the thrum in her head the song had awakened. Aunt May's humming had stopped, but the rhythm stayed with her. It echoed faintly in her ribcage like a heartbeat out of time.

The old Gemfields stretched before her in brittle gold and dark shadow. Rusted machinery jutted from the earth like old bones. A tailings pile shimmered in the dying light. Somewhere out there was the trench Kael had marked earlier in the week, the site where they'd found the pulse-readings and half-buried sapphires that sparked.

Ella reached the ridge and sat on a sun-warmed boulder, letting her breath even out. Below, Kael's figure was already there, crouched down in the already pre-dug pit. He'd spread out his equipment with scientific precision: a battered journal, a solar lantern and a selection of small instruments designed for soil reading and frequency logging. He hadn't seen her yet.

She watched him for a moment, purely out of curiosity. In the half-light, he looked slightly younger. More earnest. He no longer looked like the man trying to tame the unknown with data points but more like a little boy chasing constellations that no one else could see. And part of her softened. She stood and made her way down the slope.

Kael looked up at her arrival; he gave a nod that wasn't quite a smile.

"You came."

"I felt the stone shift," she said simply, tapping her pouch.

"Me too," he replied.

"Something's...building." The scrub behind them rustled faintly. A breeze kicked up, warm at first, then strangely cold. The light was almost gone now, the sky a beautiful, bruised violet. Kael picked up one of the sapphires, holding it flat in his palm. It glimmered, soft as breath.

The scrub smelled of iron and dust, the night air thick with heat that wouldn't quite leave. Ella crouched beside Kael and their torches cut to narrow beams. Spread across the dirt between them, there was a handful of sapphires that pulsed faintly like coals in a dying fire. Kael had laid them out in a careful pattern, muttering measurements as though he could keep the universe honest by writing it down. His notebook lay open on his knee; pages smeared with graphite sketches of grids and nodes.

"Ready?" he asked.

Ella's fingers brushed the pouch at her chest.

"Not really."

He gave a tight smile.

"Good...That's healthy." He placed the last stone. For a heartbeat nothing happened. Just a circle of dusty gems, a scientist's nervous breath - a miner's sceptical squint. Then the air shifted. The sapphires pulsed together, light threading between them, faint lines sketching themselves in blue fire across the dirt. Ella gasped. The lines connected in neat angles, forming a lattice that hovered just above the ground, a mesh of light bending with impossible precision. It wasn't random. It was perfect architecture.

Kael's face lit up in the glow, his eyes wide.

"It's a projection," he whispered in awe.

"The stones are linked. Data nodes maybe. This must be the network beneath us."

Ella reached out instinctively. The nearest line of light curved toward her hand like a snake to heat. Her fingers tingled as though brushing static. For a moment, the lattice dented under her touch, a ripple spreading outward until the entire mesh quivered. The air thrummed as images flashed across the lattice too fast to parse, like frames of film skipped in jittering succession. A country town street she didn't know, a woman crying into a mirror, a city skyline freezing mid-collapse and then her own face, doubled with eyes wide in terror. She jerked back, clutching her hand to her chest. The lattice stilled, its glow steady once more.

"Oh my! You're resonating with it," Kael said, voice awed.

"You're not just seeing it; you're like somehow a part of its language or something."

"Don't," Ella snapped.

"Don't bring me into your experiments."

He looked at her, sternly.

"Ella, this…this is bigger than us. Much bigger. These arrays could extend across the continent. Maybe even the world. If we can map them…"

"We?" she shot back stopping him from going any further.

"And what about the men with rifles? The ones who want to take this all away from us?"

Kael hesitated. His silence was answer enough.

A sound cut through the night, a low hum, not from the stones but from the ground itself. The lattice brightened, casting harsh light across the scrub. And then Aunt May's voice rose on the wind. A chant, low and rhythmic, weaving through the hum. The lattice responded, the lines shifting, reconfiguring, nodes flaring like stars. Ella's breath caught.

'She's controlling it, she must be."

"No," Kael whispered.

"I don't think so, I think she's remembering it."

The mesh rose higher, stretching upward into the air, columns of light spiralling into a dome above them. For an instant Ella saw the entire night sky replaced by a wireframe. Stars pinned neatly at intersections, the Milky Way re-ordered into geometry.

Her knees went weak. She pressed her hands to the dirt to steady herself. The sapphire in her pouch pulsed hard enough to hurt.

Kael stared, transfixed.

"What if…no…But maybe this just might be the *operating system* of reality." The chant faded out, and the dome collapsed into silence, leaving only the faint glow of the stones.

Ella panted, heart hammering.

"If so," she said hoarsely,

"we're standing on it. And I think someone's trying to hack it."

Kael closed his notebook slowly, reverently.

"No, Ella. Someone already has."

For a long moment, neither of them moved. The afterglow of the lattice shimmered across his face, catching in the hollows beneath his eyes, softening the sharpness that had lived there for weeks. He looked…almost human again. Vulnerable, like the light had stripped away the armour he wore for the job.

She realised she was still breathing hard, their shoulders were almost touching. The silence between them wasn't comfortable, it hummed with everything they hadn't said. He turned toward her, eyes reflecting the dying blue light.

"You shouldn't have touched it," he said quietly. But the words came out wrong, gentler than a reprimand, almost a soft plea.

Ella gave a half-smile, faint and tired.

"What are you talking about? You'd have done the same."

He hesitated.

"Yeah. But it would've killed me."

She held his gaze, pulse still racing. For a moment the world shrank to the narrow space between them, into the dust, the heat and the pulse of something ancient still ticking beneath the earth. Then Kael blinked and looked away, breaking the spell.

"Come on," he said softly.

"Before the grid decides to reboot."

Ella nodded, but her hand brushed his as they rose, fingers grazing just long enough to leave a static spark that wasn't expected.

*
**

The path back toward camp felt longer than usual. The sapphire lay heavy against her chest; its earlier pulse now dulled to a steady warmth as if sleeping. The night air had cooled, but her skin still carried the residue of light and static. Every few steps, Ella glanced behind her, half-expecting to see Kael following. But she was alone.

Her boots crunched over the ridge gravel. In the distance, the neighbour's generator hummed its low, familiar tune, but it felt out of place now. As if it belonged to a version of reality that she'd just stepped sideways from.

Above her, the stars had returned to their natural scatter, however Ella saw them very differently now. The grid was gone, yes, but its imprint remained in her mind like an afterimage burn that you get when you look at a bright light. She imagined reaching up, pinching one star between two fingers and dragging it back to the intersection it had fallen from.

The chant still echoed faintly in her mind as she reached her caravan, stepped inside and clicked the lock quietly. The space was small, but familiar. A bed crammed along one wall. Shelves with scattered notebooks, quartz chunks, bits of tin and wire she hadn't thrown out yet. Her old lantern cast a soft, flickering glow that made the shadows ripple.

Ella sat on the edge of her mattress and peeled off her

boots, muscles aching in places she hadn't known she used. She opened the pouch slowly and tipped the sapphire into her palm. It was dark now, inert, but she could feel it watching her or maybe…it was listening. She lay back, stone resting on her chest.

Sleep didn't come. Not properly, instead, she slipped into something between a dream and a download. In the dark, images fired behind her closed eyes, too fast to focus, the wireframe sky. Kael's breath caught in awe and Aunt May's song threading the air like a key turning in a lock. And then…the earth cracked open beneath her, not literally, but in memory.

She saw an ancient mineshaft collapsing in reverse with its timbers rising, dust flying upward and the stones reseating themselves perfectly like chess pieces. At the centre of the restored shaft there was a smooth black structure. Obsidian-like, it was humming and had a geometric light. It didn't appear to be built, instead, it looked placed there.

Voices rose, but they didn't sound human, perhaps more like data-patterned in way that it might be a language spoken in encryption. And somewhere in that weave, was her name. *Ella.*

She jolted upright.

The air in the caravan was still. Outside, something scraped softly across the outer wall. Once. Then silence.

She held her breath, eyes fixed on the door. Then came the whisper, so quiet it could have been the wind, but wasn't. It sounded like

‘Not just a witness.” Her blood chilled.

She clutched the stone hard in her hand and stared out the tiny caravan window. Nothing moved. But in the moonlit dust outside, just before the breeze stirred it away there was a single, perfect footprint. Facing the caravan.

echo sync initiated...

CHAPTER EIGHT
GLOBAL COLLAPSE

The heat hit early. By 7am the sun was already burning through the caravan walls like one of those government searchlights, waking Ella with a slow roast to the face. She groaned, rolled over, and smacked her pillow like it had betrayed her. Somewhere outside, a kookaburra was gargling its strange song.

She dragged herself upright, hair a mess, shirt stuck to her back with sleep-sweat. The dream had evaporated the moment her eyes opened, but her fingers instinctively reached for the sapphire pouch at her neck. Still there. Still warm. Outside, the hill was already alive, neighbours with bad coffee and half-argued theories.

Kael was out by the water tank on the old, abandoned claim behind hers. He looked like he was trying to coax it into delivering something that resembled a shower from a garden hose. After making a cup of coffee, Ella slipped on her boots and made her way over to him.

"You look like a toasted moth," he said teasingly as she approached.

"I feel like one," Ella agreed.

"Is that water or steam you're bathing in there?"

Kael aimed the hose vaguely in her direction, splashing her arm.

"You tell me," he asked playfully.

She flinched.

"Oh god! ... bloody hell... it's both."

"Good for the skin," he said with a grin.

"Kael, it's bloody-well boiling brine filtered through fossilised possum fur, not bloody skincare," she shot back, and he grinned. The hill always felt more alive before the weight of the world settled in on everyone.

"Still want to check that fault line later?" he asked.

"Yeah, sure..." Ella said.

"But only if we can make a stop for lunch that doesn't involve baked beans or powdered eggs."

Kael held up a can with a rusted label.

"Too late," he laughed.

After breakfast and a short walk to check the cracked ridge sensor - mostly uneventful, apart from Kael falling into a ditch and accusing a wallaby of sabotage. They returned to Ella's claim to find chaos unfolding. Aunt May was in the middle of her camp kitchen, waving a wooden spoon at a fully grown hen that had apparently decided to move in.

"You reincarnated bugger!" Aunt May shouted.

"You think I don't see you watching the voltage? Get

back in your bloody timeline!" The chook clucked once, turned calmly, and strutted off into the bush.

"This place is going crazy," Kael said, blinking.

"Did she just say… timeline?"

"She did," Ella confirmed, not missing a beat.

"Last week she yelled at a kookaburra for 'looping the laugh track too early."

"You know," Kael said, eyes wide,

"she might actually be the only sane one here."

It wasn't until later that afternoon, after the sun dipped low enough to turn the red dust golden and the air cooled to something breathable, that Ella suggested they walk into town.

"I wouldn't mind a glass of wine or two," she announced.

Kael looked up from his sketchbook, surprised.

"You?"

"Yeah, I earned it," she said.

"I've sweated, hallucinated, argued with a solar panel, and survived Aunt May's quantum poultry… that deserves at least one pint, surely." He concluded.

The Rubyvale Hotel was already alive with end-of-day noise. Fossickers, miners, and tourists all clumped around mismatched tables. The air was thick with pub chips, cigarette smoke, and sunburnt gossip. Even the fans rotated lazily overhead as if even they couldn't be bothered to make the next rotation. Then there was Mick's battered old TV that was mounted at a crooked angle near the bar. It was already playing some city news broadcast that no one was paying attention to.

Ella leaned against the bar beside Kael as Mick poured them two local lagers with the solemnity of a priest delivering sacraments.

"You lot been out by the ridge?" he asked, eyes narrowed.

Kael nodded in response.

"Sensors still flaring." Mick grunted.

"Yeah, mate. Something's off, eh? My compass spun this morning like it was drunk. Then went dead. And the fridge in the kitchen defrosted... only backwards."

Ella frowned.

"Wait...What...Backwards?"

"Yep. Put a warm steak in. Came out frozen solid ten minutes later. Still bleeding." Mick continued.

Kael gave a low whistle.

"Wow, okay...That's a new one." They barely had time to laugh before the first footage came on.

"Hey," Mick shouted to get everyone's attention.

Ella stood with Kael among a half-circle of miners, the air stale with sweat and dust, everyone staring at the flickering screen. A reporter in Sydney spoke fast over shaky handheld video. Behind her, a skyscraper shimmered as if underwater. Windows bent, floors sagged like soft wax, then snapped back into place with a sound the microphone couldn't catch. Cars on the street below duplicated in stuttering pairs before collapsing into one another, drivers screaming from both mouths at once.

"Unconfirmed reports..." the reporter's voice cracked with static

"The Australian government is urging calm; power grid interruptions are linked to..." Then the feed froze. The reporter's face doubled, then tripled, eyes staring in three directions. The screen went black.

Mick spat into a rag.

"Bugger me!"

Kael's jaw was tight, knuckles white on the bar.

"It's spreading."

Ella felt the sapphire pouch pulse against her chest like a heartbeat too strong for one body. The broadcast cut back. Now it was London. Big Ben's hands spinning in opposite directions at once, crowds screaming as the tower flickered between daylight and night. Then New York, Times Square screens blurring into grids, pedestrians splitting into mirror-selves before recombining mid-stride. Then Tokyo, trains arriving twice at once, passengers pouring from both versions into the same platform until they overlapped like bad animation.

The room was silent but for the low hum of the TV.

"End of times," exclaimed Old Stan.

"Or some bloody fool's science project has gone horribly wrong."

A hand touched Ella's arm. And she jumped, Aunt May had appeared soundlessly, eyes heavy with knowledge older than the dirt under their boots. "The song is out of balance," she said softly.

"The stones are calling louder than they should be."

Ella turned to her, not really knowing what any of this meant.

"What happens if it keeps spreading?" she whispered.

"The world forgets itself," Aunt May said.

"And when the forgetting is complete, it begins again. Fresh. Empty." She smiled.

Reboot. The word shuddered through Ella's mind. Aunt May hadn't said it, but Ella couldn't help wondering if that's what was happening.

Kael cleared his throat, eyes still on the screen.

"There's another possibility. What if the network can be overridden to prevent it from going into a restart..."

"Overridden?" Ella echoed. Completely shocked at what she had just heard Kael say.

"Think of it like editing code, while the program's still running," Kael said. "It's dangerous and unstable but it would preserve continuity. It would keep us intact."

"And if we fail?" Ella whispered, confused.

Kael didn't answer. He didn't need to. The images on the pub TV said everything. Cities stuttering, shadows moving before their owners and the skies fracturing into invisible grids that no one else seemed to notice until it was all too late.

Someone near the bar shouted,

"Bloody CGI," but his voice shook when he said it. Mick turned up the volume, but it didn't help. The footage glitched in real time now. Buildings flickering between states. A street in New York where the pavement folded up like paper. In Tokyo, a train entered a station twice. In Sydney, that mirrored skyscraper shimmered like it was being rendered again from scratch.

Kael's knuckles were white around his beer glass. Then he stood without a word and walked out the side door. Ella didn't follow right away. She watched him vanish into the night, his figure bending slightly at the edges, like the world wasn't sure where to place him anymore. People kept talking, but their voices sounded somewhat distant now like they were detached. Somewhere, Aunt May's voice echoed from her seat by the window, soft and grim.

"Once the lattice remembers you, it never lets go."

Ella's spine chilled. She set her drink down, left the circle of murmuring miners, and stepped out into the evening air.

She found Kael outside, leaning against the far edge of the veranda's corner bar. The light was low outside, the sky purpled and bruised and the cicadas humming their restless code through the town. He didn't look up when she approached.

"You saw what Aunt May meant tonight," he said, his voice rough.

"The choice isn't theirs; and it isn't mine." He turned, eyes dark and restless in the twilight.

"It's you, Ella. You're the only one who can touch the lattice without it tearing."

She stopped a few feet away, arms crossed tightly,

"That's not comforting," she said.

"It's not meant to be." Kael shot back. He exhaled, slowly.

"Whatever this is, it's been building for longer than we thought. Maybe even longer than anyone knows. The grid in the sky, the synced dream patterns and even Aunt May's chants, they're not isolated incidents."

Ella shook her head.

"I didn't ask for this, you know. I didn't come here to

be well-chosen or whatever you want to call it."

"I know," Kael said softly.

"But it's happening anyway, whether you like it or not."

They stood there in silence as the last edge of light vanished behind the trees in the distance and the landscape dipped in a bruised amber. The buzz of the pub faded away behind them. And for a moment, Ella felt like she could still see the lines, very faint and humming just beneath the sky. The lattice wasn't gone. It was waiting.

She shook her head.

"I'm not anyone's chosen key. I'm just..."

"You're not just," he interrupted. His voice softening.

"You must be the bridge. That's why that shadow figure found you. That's why the chants answer you. And that's why the government will probably do anything to take you if they find out."

By the time Ella walked back to her caravan, the town had settled into a hush, the kind of quiet that wasn't peace, but pressure. She passed a few locals still on the pub veranda, their voices lower now, words short and nervous. Someone coughed. Someone else laughed too loud. But no one dared to mention the news. No one ever did talk about things when they were that kind of strange.

The stars were bright overhead, crisp in the way only outback skies could manage. Too bright, if she was honest. Every constellation looked slightly out of place like they'd been rearranged just enough to be noticed by someone who knew them.

Her boots kicked softly at the dust. Each step echoed more than it should have. She paused briefly to check the generator hum in the distance. Still going. The caravan park's low glow spilled just far enough to make her feel like the edge of the world wasn't swallowing her whole. Ella noticed how it smelled faintly of eucalyptus soap and red dust as she walked past.

Getting back to her caravan, Ella dropped her pouch gently on the counter, the sapphire inside clinking once against the metal zipper. She poured herself a half-glass of water from the bottle that sat on the edge of her bed and stared at her boots. Everything felt heavier. Not just her limbs, but the air, the choices, the knowledge. Her hands were shaking before she noticed.

She clenched her fists, then let them go. Lying down, she curled onto her side, listening to the sound of distant cicadas filling the night. Somewhere out there, Kael was probably staring at the sky, trying to sketch a pattern out of chaos and Aunt May was probably singing to the grid. Ella closed her eyes… not to sleep, but to rest in the darkness a moment, to take it all in.

That night, the Gemfields felt smaller than usual. The floodlights beamed over the government camp, the soldiers tense and their radios crackling with sharp voices. Ella walked the edge of her claim, sapphire clutched in her fist, listening to the silence between cicadas. Every now and then the world seemed to hiccup. The stars shifting slightly, as though re-pinned to different coordinates. As if on cue, a spotlight swept across the claim, lingering too long. Ella's heart thudded. The world wasn't just cracking, it was watching.

01001101 01000101 01001101 01001111 01010010 01011001

"Some names
are written into the ground,
not onto paper."

The air in Rubyvale felt heavier than it should, and the sky felt like it was pressing down on the outback. Ella hadn't slept. She sat outside her caravan at dawn, elbows on her knees, the sapphire pouch warm against her chest, waiting for the world to decide if it was going to shatter or not.

She'd watched the news cycle repeat itself into static the night before with cityscapes bending, multiplying and vanishing. Skyscrapers flickering like half-finished thoughts. People speaking over themselves in doubled voices. Trains entering stations twice, children disappearing mid-frame and returning as if nothing had happened. Every screen had a different glitch, but the same feel. Something fundamental had been exposed. Something not meant to be seen. The world looked like it had gone crazy. The world had suddenly changed in that moment, but Ella suspected it hadn't started changing then. It had only just been revealed.

She stared out at the dirt track winding past the fence, wondering what it must've been like to see that footage in a place where the sky was full of towers instead of stars. What happened in Rubyvale was quite tense, sure, but restrained. But in Sydney? London? Sao Paulo?

She imagined a young woman in New York standing in her kitchen, coffee halfway to her lips, watching her own apartment fold inside out on the morning news. Or a commuter in Tokyo who saw the train he'd just gotten off pull into the same platform again with the same people. Twice. What would it feel like for a billion people to simultaneously question the floor beneath their feet? Not just fear, but uncertainty. That corrosive doubt that makes everything you rely on from traffic lights, shadows, to your own reflection feel suspect.

By now, Ella was certain there'd be civil unrest. Power grids failing from the panic alone. Banks freezing withdrawals for investigation. Religious leaders claiming revelation. Scientists issuing measured press statements that couldn't explain a single frame. Governments would scramble to contain it, to rationalise it.

There would be gas leaks, solar flares and perhaps even advanced cyberattack and shared hallucination from unregulated media. But Ella had seen the lattice. She had touched it. This wasn't code leaking into nature. It was nature revealing its code to us.

She rubbed the pouch absently, the sapphire inside pressing back like a heartbeat. Aunt May had been calm throughout it all, sipping her tea and humming that impossible melody. Kael had gone quiet, caught between awe and terror. But Ella? She didn't feel chosen. She felt trapped. As if she'd been walking through her life thinking she was on a dirt path only to realise it was a pressure plate. Now something had triggered it and the world, all of it, was about to respond.

Meanwhile, down the hill further, in his makeshift camp, Kael emerged from his tent, rumpled and restless. He poured black coffee into a blue and white speckled enamel mug and sipped on it slowly, staring out across the scrub with the eyes of someone still trying to reconcile dreams from data.

The air smelled of dry grass, sweat, and scorched metal. His notebook lay open on the camp table, pages half-smudged with graphite lines drawn in the dark fragmented sketches of the lattice, intersecting angles overlaid with human silhouettes. The more he tried to map it, the less it made sense. There was something about the way the grid moved defied physics. It didn't behave like a projection, or energy, matter even. It reacted more like a thought. An instinctive, invisible nervous system flickering beneath the surface of the planet and somehow Ella was the only one who could touch it without triggering a feedback loop.

He rubbed the back of his neck, glancing up toward

her caravan on the ridge. He knew she hadn't slept. Neither had he. They were both running on adrenaline, coffee, and something far older: the kind of knowing you didn't get from instruments or lectures. He took another sip of coffee and tapped the side of his mug, as if hoping it might shake loose some clarity. But the only answer it offered was the soft hum of cicadas, warming up ready for another blistering day. Then...another sound-faint. Subterranean. Familiar. Kael's head snapped toward the east. Not again, he thought. Not this early.

Kael froze, mug halfway to his lips. The low hum in the earth pulsed again subtle, but undeniable. He reached for the portable radio on the table. An old HF model, patched together with electrical tape and a bit of faith. Most days, it picked up nothing but weather updates and slow-talking outback truckers. But today, it was already crackling. He adjusted the frequency dial. The static stuttered, then cleared just enough for a voice to push through.

"...repeating, this is Alice Springs regional relay on HF-band emergency override. We are experiencing an unprecedented interruption across national systems. Authorities urge citizens to remain indoors and limit device usage to essential..."

The signal faltered, whined high, then stabilised.

142

"Satellite positioning anomalies confirmed. Air traffic in eastern states has been grounded as a precaution. The Prime Minister is expected to..." static crack "...global coordination task force has been initiated alongside emergency scientific advisors."

Kael's grip tightened. A beat of silence, then another voice took over, this one was shaking and much younger.

"Uh...this is Dr. Anika Sen, field consultant at Canberra ARC. If you're receiving this broadcast, know that we're aware of the distortion fields being reported. They appear to correlate with geomagnetic anomalies and with a pattern we don't yet understand...If you've witnessed visual or auditory irregularities, especially repeating sequences, mirrored structures, or..." the voice paused, faltering "duplicate individuals...please report to your nearest..." crackle

"We are not calling this a simulation failure. Repeat. We are not calling this a..." signal loss.

Kael clicked the radio off. He stood perfectly still, heart hammering. "Duplicate individuals? he wondered. The phrase echoed like a stone dropped down a mineshaft. He looked up toward the ridge again. Time to find Ella.

Kael didn't wait to pack up. He grabbed his notebook, stuffed it into his bag with the half-finished

sketches, and took off up the path toward the ridge. He found Ella already outside her caravan, pacing. She must've felt it too, the low frequency shifting through the earth like something alive, like something was waking up.

She looked up the moment he approached, reading his face before he spoke. His eyes darted toward the horizon, then back.

"We should move tonight," he said quietly.

"Before they tighten the cordon."

Ella nodded. She had no questions; there was no need to question it.

The convoy had doubled in size overnight. Tan-coloured trucks now lined the far track near the edge of the scrub, and soldiers patrolled the ridgeline with rifles angled downward, but their eyes kept flicking to the ground, as if they feared what lay beneath more than any of us miners.

Kael stood beside her, arms folded tight. The soft morning light glinted off the rim of his mug, long forgotten on the ground.

"They're not just here for security," he said.

"They're waiting for confirmation. Once they have it, they'll close the zone. Lock it down like they have with other sites."

Ella didn't speak. The sapphire at her chest pulsed, once.

"They know someone triggered the lattice," Kael added.

"And they're narrowing it down."

She turned to him, searching his face.

"How do you know that?"

He hesitated, jaw flexing.

"Because I would. If I were them." A silence settled between them. The kind that always came before hard choices. Ella looked up the ridge again. The soldiers moved with the tension of people who'd seen too much and understood too little. Even their boots avoided the darker patches of earth. Kael stepped a little closer.

"We leave tonight. Just you, me, and whatever you've been carrying since that night."

Ella's fingers brushed the edge of the pouch beneath her shirt.

"If it comes to it..., can we even get out?"

Kael's voice was low.

"We won't be going via the roads." He wandered off to check the edge of the camp, leaving Ella with a growing hum behind her ribs and no clear way forward. She ducked back into her caravan, partly to escape the soldiers' stares and partly to escape the weight of Kael's words.

Inside, the air was warm and still. A breeze stirred the

curtain only slightly, just enough to lift the smell of dust and eucalyptus soap. She moved on autopilot folding a shirt, tucking away an old book, straightening the chipped enamel mug on the bench. Until something caught her eye.

Wedged between two notebooks was a small, creased photo. She hadn't noticed it in weeks. She picked it up carefully. It was her and her dad, back before he passed away, both grinning with sunburnt faces and gemstone dust across their arms. He was holding up a sapphire the size of his thumbnail like he'd just caught a fish on Moreton Island, and she was laughing. She remembered how light everything had felt that day. No grids. No hums. Just sweat and dirt and the stubborn hope that maybe they'd strike a good seam. She swallowed hard. Folded the photo and tucked it into the pouch with the stone.

"Just you and me now," she whispered, not sure if she meant her father or the gem. A gust of wind rocked the caravan slightly, and she looked up, tense again. Outside, the sky was bluer than it had any right to be. Like it was overcompensating. She stepped out into the light again just as Kael reappeared around the side of the hut, nodding grimly. Then came the footsteps.

"Ella!"

She turned.

Old Tommy stood there, mouth dry and eyes wide. He held his battered hat in both hands, twisting it like he meant to wring the truth out of it.

"You've got one of the stones, don't you?" he blurted.

"Ella." Came a voice behind her. Ella stiffened.

"Why?"

"Please," he said, desperate.

"They've got my brother in one of the trucks. Said he touched something, and now he's sick. They won't let me see him. If you give them your stone, maybe they'll trade."

Kael rose sharply.

"Tommy…"

But Ella's gut clenched. She saw the way Tommy wouldn't meet her eyes, the way his shoulders hunched as if already guilty. The sound of boots behind him confirmed it.

Soldiers poured around the caravan, rifles raised. Mirrored Woman stepped forward, sunglasses gleaming with the sunrise.

"Thank you, Mr. Davis," she said smoothly. Tommy flinched at the use of his surname. Ella's hand darted to her pouch, but a soldier was faster. The butt of his rifle cracked against her temple. The world whited out.

She woke in motion. The world was metal and

147

rumble. Every bump in the road jarred her bones. A steady, low engine hummed beneath her, layered with the occasional rattle of something unsecured metal on metal, tools maybe. Her wrists ached. Bound tight. She shifted, wrists burning, chest heaving. The pouch…was gone.

Panic flared hot in her throat. Not just for the stone, but for what it meant to be separated from it. Like her spine had been unplugged from something vital. Across from her, Kael sat shackled too, his head low, a split on his lip crusted with dried blood. His wrists were bound to a metal bar welded to the floor. He saw her stir and lifted his eyes. Just enough to meet hers. He gave a tiny, deliberate shake of his head… don't speak.

Ella's breath caught. She swallowed it. The truck jolted hard, throwing her against the wall. Her shoulder hit steel. Suspension groaned. The interior was dim, lit only by narrow slats along the upper walls, crude, barred windows that let in strips of morning light. Through one of them, she caught a glimpse of red earth sliding past. Then the ridgeline. And beyond it, floodlights. White, surgical beams angled downward over the scrub. They weren't lighting up a road or an equipment compound. They were focused inward, into the earth itself.

She saw black tents. Temporary structures. Military. Cables running in grid-like patterns over the ground. People in hazmat suits. Antennae. Surveillance rigs.

And at the very centre was a circle of scaffolding and a deep cut into the ground.

"That is the lattice site." she realised,

"They found it." Ella's breath turned as cold as ice.

Kael met her gaze again, only tighter now. Focused. Not fear. Not surprise. But Confirmation. They weren't prisoners. They were evidence. She clenched her jaw. Not here. Not now. She needed to save the reaction for later. Another jolt. And the truck began to slow then the brakes hissed.

Kael shifted slightly, using the sound to murmur under his breath: "They know it was you. That's why we're not dead."

The truck jolted, suspension groaning and through slatted windows, Ella glimpsed the ridge sliding past. Beyond it, floodlights beamed over what looked to be inside the government camp. They were driven inside a tented structure that smelled of ozone and antiseptic. When the doors opened, the sound hit her first: screams. Not loud. Not human. A chorus of pain distorted through static.

They were shoved out into the glare of halogen lamps, boots scuffing across temporary flooring that had the echo of a warehouse but smelled like sterilised panic.

Ella blinked hard. The light was blinding after the

dark of the truck, but what came into view made her stomach twist. Cots. Dozens of them. Maybe more, lined up like a medical ward slapped together by someone with funding but no soul.

Each cot held a body. There were men, women, soldiers, and local miners. None of them moved like they should.

Sapphire shards, small, jagged slivers, had been embedded into their chests. Not surgically. But forced, pressed into them as if someone had tried to plug them in. The skin around their wounds seemed to be bruised and strangely mottled, with dark veins spidering outward like cracks in ceramic.

And then the glow…blue and cold. A heartbeat rhythm pulsed from the stones to their skin, making their torsos rise and fall in the most shallow, unnatural patterns.

Some of them twitched their heads jerking slightly out of sync with their bodies and their limbs fluttering like old VHS tape trying to stabilise. Others lay perfectly still, eyes glassy but glowing faint blue beneath the lids. Like the lights were on, but no one was home. Or worse…like as if someone else was. Ella gagged, swallowing it back with a noise that wasn't entirely human.

'This is new," Kael mused standing beside her, tone grim but dry.

"I don't recall seeing this in the brochure."

Ella shot him a look.

"I wonder, was this the deluxe package, or the bonus content?"

Their guards didn't respond. Didn't even flinch. They just pushed them forward again, toward a cordoned-off area marked with yellow hazard tape and an overuse of acronyms.

"Welcome to Glitch Camp," Ella whispered under her breath.

"Where the rooms come with trauma and a free existential crisis."

Kael's eyes darted from cot to cot.

"They're testing integration," his voice was clipped. Controlled.

"They look like they're trying to embed the stones directly to see who resonates. And...who fractures."

"And these poor bastards?" Ella gasped.

"Beta testers. Willing or not," He responded, still in awe of what he was seeing.

A man on the nearest cot spasmed suddenly, arching off the mattress, a high keening sound escaping his throat as the stone in his chest flared like a live wire. For a moment, his mouth moved independently of his face, like it was catching up. Ella took a step back.

"Nope. Nope, I'm good. Let's go back to the truck.

That hellbox looks positively cozy compared to this shitshow."

Kael didn't smile. But his fingers brushed hers briefly. Ella wasn't sure if it was for reassurance, or as a warning. They were being watched. Not just by the guards. And not by the people still twitching. Something else in the room felt aware they were there. Like the lattice had eyes now.

The Mirrored Woman walked between the cots as if they were exhibits. "Early trials," she said calmly.

"Unstable at present. But promising."

"They're dying," Ella choked in complete disbelief.

"Not dying, they're adapting," the woman corrected. She turned her head slightly, glasses catching the light.

"Your stone stabilises the interface. You touched it without disintegration. That makes you…how do I put this…unique."

Ella lunged at her, but the shackles pulled her down. The soldiers didn't even flinch.

Kael's voice was ragged.

"You don't understand what you're tampering with. If you force the resonance…"

"…we control it," the Mirrored Woman finished. "Australia cannot afford to let others take control over this. Just think what our country's army could do with reality itself."

Ella's stomach dropped. Soldiers. Weapons. Entire nations glitching like the roo she saw down on Zircon Avenue, like Mrs. Dalloway doubling and like the soldier who screamed twice.

"No," she whispered.

"You'll break everything."

The woman tilted her head, as if curious.

"No, we'll learn it, we'll remake it."

She nodded once. A soldier lifted Ella roughly, dragging her toward a row of empty cots. A sapphire shard gleamed on the tray beside it, humming faintly. Ella fought, twisting, but the stone in her pouch was gone. She was bare and helpless. The cot straps squealed as they reached for her wrists. And then the lights stuttered. The halogens buzzed, flared, died.

They were herded past the last row of cots, toward a folding table covered in data pads, wires, and half-sanitised instruments that looked like they'd been stolen from both a battlefield and a dentist's office. Kael slowed, eyes narrowing.

"That's resonance monitoring gear."

Ella didn't ask how he knew. She'd stopped wanting answers the usual way.

A figure appeared at the edge of her vision, tall, with a coat too clean for the dust, clipboard in one hand and stylus in the other. Not military. Not quite civilian either, more science-bureaucrat chic. He didn't look up. "We're accelerating trials," he said flatly, as if they were just new additions to a spreadsheet.

"You'll be taken to Intake for calibration."

"Calibration," Ella repeated.

"Wonderful. Do we get lunch with that?"

The man glanced at her briefly but carefully measured.

"You're the one who touched it."

Ella's mouth went dry.

Kael shifted closer instinctively.

"She doesn't know anything."

But the man was already looking past them, waving a hand toward the curtained area near the far wall.

And then…a whisper, not from the guards, not from Kael and not from the nearest cot.

"…Ella…" came her name. Soft and drawn out like breath fogging glass. Ella froze.

The woman on the bed hadn't moved. Still glassy-eyed, still glowing faintly blue. But her lips had parted, and a trickle of blue light pooled beneath her lower lip like drool from another dimension.

"…Ella…reset protocol…"

Ella stepped back fast, hitting Kael's side.

"Did you hear that?"

"I heard," He whispered back.

The guards didn't react. Either they hadn't noticed, or

they were used to it.

The woman twitched again, her spine arching just enough to lift the crystal embedded in her chest. It pulsed once strangely in sync with Ella's pouch. Even from this distance, without the stone, she felt it. A tug. A recognition.

'She's in there," Ella whispered.

"Whoever she was… part of her is still inside."

The man with the clipboard turned sharply now, interested. But Ella didn't give him the satisfaction of asking anything. Instead, she leaned over the woman's cot just enough to whisper

"Hang on. I'm going to find a way to pull you out."

The woman twitched again, a single tear or maybe code slipping down her cheek. Then her body went still. Her eyes stayed open, glowing faintly. The guards moved them on.

Ella didn't resist this time. She didn't need to be told anymore. This wasn't a camp, it was an interface, and someone was already logged in.

For a moment the entire camp went black. In the dark, a voice echoed near her ear: fractured, doubled, glitching.

"Remember the grid," it was the voice of the shadowy figure, that felt more like an insider. The lights snapped back. The soldiers cursed, looking around. For an instant

Ella's shackles lay open. Yet no one had touched them.

She bolted. Kael staggered after her, guards shouting, rifles raised. They ran between cots of half-crystallised victims, screams and static filling the air. Ella's heart pounded, feet sliding in dust. Behind her, a soldier shouted:

'Don't let the girl escape!'

Ahead, the night air split open. Aunt May's chant cut across the chaos, steady and resonant, louder than rifles. The lattice flickered in Ella's vision, glowing faint over the camp. She reached for it with everything she had left. And the sapphire, though stolen, pulsed once in her chest.

✲✲ 01001100 01100001 01110100 01110100 01101001
01100011 01100101 ✲✲

CHAPTER TEN
THE DREAMTIME KEY

They, ran until the hum of the camp fell behind them and the scrub closed like a scar over their path. Branches slapped against arms and shins. Dry grass crackled beneath their boots, the sound too loud in the open dark. The floodlights were long gone now, swallowed by the curve of the ridge and the black canopy overhead. No stars, just the blind throb of breath and effort.

The night breathed hot and metallic, cicadas shouting in pulses that made Ella think of code compiled in sound. There was a rhythm to it that was too precise, too patterned, like the land was translating something ancient into binary through insect song. Kael stumbled once on a root, caught himself, kept going. He didn't swear. He didn't stop. Neither of them did. There was no time for pain. No room for questions. The words would come later, if there was a later.

Ella's lungs burned. Her throat felt scoured raw, the back of her neck damp with sweat and fear. She clutched the pouch now missing the stone. She clutched it so tightly that her knuckles had gone numb. She hadn't dared ask Kael how she had gotten the pouch back during the chaos. She didn't want to break the momentum.

They wove deeper into the bush, the terrain familiar now in the way only trauma can teach. Every turn was a remembered footfall; every tree, a shadow half-seen in sleep. When the earth finally dipped into a hollow, they slowed. Kael hunched, hands on knees, panting. Ella doubled over beside him, breath shaking in and out. For a moment there was only the heat of their bodies and the sound of the world waiting. Then a glow found them between the bloodwoods. No torch. No floodlight. Just a small, patient shimmer of moonlight caught in water. They turned toward it at the same time.

Aunt May stood by a circle of stones set into the dirt, her silhouette both sharp and dissolving in the light. Her hands were open, palms up. Her voice moved low through the air, quiet and resonant, a chant Ella had heard thread through the lattice once before. The sound unspooled, reshaping the silence.

"Here," Aunt May said, and it was as if the word itself carved a place into the world that hadn't existed before. It *was* like she had been waiting for them.

Ella hovered at the edge of the circle, dust clinging to her arms, the pouch warm against her chest. Her feet wanted to move, but something older held her still. She had trusted Aunt May once. Her stories, her tea, and her fire-lit riddles when the generator failed. Those stories had felt like myth, harmless folklore filed under family. But now they had teeth. The woman before her wasn't just an elder with river-stone bones and sharp opinions. She was part of this. A keeper of something no one had warned Ella she'd inherit. What if stepping into the circle meant surrendering more than control? What if the lattice saw her and decided she didn't belong?

Aunt May's chanting never wavered, steady as water smoothing stone. Kael waited, eyes on Ella, chest still heaving from the run. He knew better than to speak. The ring of rocks shimmered faintly, dust caught in their grooves like static woven into geometry. Ella stepped forward, not from trust, but because something in her wanted to remember. Aunt May raised her palms.

"They put iron notes into a water song," she murmured,

"and wonder why it drowns."

Ella's breath snagged. The air inside the circle felt cooler, persuaded to stand back and watch.

Ella stared down at the ring of rocks. They weren't just placed. They were aligned. Mathematically. Dreamily. Dust had gathered in the grooves between them in deliberate patterns, the lines shimmering faintly, like static woven into geometry.

She looked once at Aunt May, who said nothing now,

only held her hands out, light brushing the creases of her palms. And then crossed the threshold. Kael followed a moment later and the circle held.

Ella and Kael stepped into the circle. What choice did they have? It felt cooler inside, as though the heat had been persuaded to stand back and watch. Aunt May nodded once to each of them, then closed her eyes and let silence gather.

"They took the stone," Ella said, breathless. She hated the fear in her voice.

Aunt May's eyes opened.

"Stones move. Songs stay."

Kael rubbed dust from his face.

"They're forcing sapphires into people, Aunt May. Soldiers and civilians alike. It's killing them."

Aunt May's gaze didn't flinch.

"It would. They put iron notes into a water song and wonder why it drowns."

She pointed at the ground between the stones. Ella followed her gesture and saw it: faint marks carved into hardpan, older than the circle. Lines, curves. A map. A lattice.

"We were given this long ago," Aunt May said.

"Not given by a man, nor a God with a beard. Given the way the world is. Our people listened. We remembered in stories because stories do not break when paper burns."

Kael crouched, breath caught.

"This...this is the same geometry we projected from the sapphires."

"Of course," Aunt May said. "The sky wears a skin. The skin breathes and sings. You saw the bones of it."

Ella knelt too, palms flat to feel the carving with her skin. The lines were shallow but undeniable, intersecting like the joinery of invisible houses. At each crossing, a small depression had been worn, as if countless fingers had pressed there to make sure it existed.

"How did you know?" Ella asked, barely above a whisper.

"We remember," Aunt May said simply.

"What others forgot. Or chose to. Every few lifetimes, the song either got too loud or too quiet, and people argued about the right way to listen to it. Sometimes they broke the drum to hear the skin better. Sometimes they set fire to the dancers," she said as she looked up at the stars.

For a moment, he stars looked pinned to a wireframe, as if freshly clicked into place.

"There were overrides," Aunt May continued.

"You might call them that. Times when the world became too thin, and we pushed, not to end it, but to ease the breath. When the balance is returned, the stories sleep."

Kael's voice came out rough.

"How did you push?"

Aunt May's mouth curved, not quite a smile.

"With what we had. Voice. Stone. One foot in the song, one in the dirt. People like you," she nodded towards Ella,

"who could carry both."

Ella's chest tightened.

"I'm not..." She stopped. The denial had worn thin; light showed through.

"The Insider man told you," Aunt May said, as if reciting something Ella should already know.

"Not all your steps were born. Some were written. That is not a curse. It is a bridge made of ribs."

Kael blinked.

"The Insider...so you've seen him?"

"Once, twice, many times," Aunt May said.

"He belongs to a story that is almost finished. He is what happens to a person when the song edits them but does not end them."

Ella thought of the way he split and recombined, how his voice lagged like words crossing a river.

"He said they'd rewrite me."

"They will try," said Aunt May.

"Machine people, paper people, gun people. They

think if they change the letters they can own the tongue," she tapped the carving.

"But this is older than their pens."

Wind lifted, smelling briefly of wet grass where no water was. The circle felt alive with attention. Ella realised, with a sudden shiver, that the attention was not only theirs. The grid listened back.

"What do we do?" Ella said. The question sounded small, but it was all she had. Aunt May knelt opposite her, hands steady over the lattice map.

"You make the key."

Kael leaned forward.

"We have the stones, Aunt May, you have some of them. They connect, yes. But the government took Ella's."

Aunt May shook her head.

"The key is not a necklace, my boy. It's a pattern in a heart."

She touched Ella lightly over the sternum. The sapphire, absent, still thrummed from the memory of where it had lain. Ella flinched, not from pain but from the intimacy of recognition, she felt it.

"Keys are not only for doors," Aunt May said.

"They're for songs, they're for tuning. You can push the lattice toward life, not erasure. But you cannot do it with metal hands. You must sing the world with your whole self. And it will sing back. If you are not steady, it will swallow you."

Kael swallowed.

"If she fails?"

"Then you will not have to worry about it," Aunt May said.

"There will be no one left to worry or worry about."

Silence again. Something in the scrub crackled. Somewhere a wallaby hopped twice, probably confused by its own echo.

"How?" Ella said at last.

"Tell me like I'm a dumb 5-year-old."

Aunt May's eyes warmed with pride, in a way that Ella hadn't expected. "Dumb people don't ask 'how.' They ask for someone else to do it for them," she smirked as she traced the map with a fingertip.

"There are nodes under this land. You woke one with your hand, my dear Ella, and another with your fear and together we will wake the rest with breath. Your breath, your voice, carries both stories of meat and of math. The chant will show you where to lean. When the lattice rises, you will press it the way you pressed the sky in your dream. Not to break it, instead to bend it like a stockman turning a herd of cattle towards a water hole."

Kael's pen hovered over his notebook, then fell useless to his lap.

"This is…beyond modelling."

"Then stop modelling," Aunt May snapped back at him.

"And start listening. Stop measuring. Start joining," She tilted her head at him.

"Your numbers will not be wasted. They will be the little stones that hold the big stones steady."

He blinked.

"You want me to…be ballast."

"I want you to be brave enough not to be the hero," Aunt May said kindly.

Ella exhaled in a soft laugh that hurt.

"And me?"

"You will be the hands that don't have hands," Aunt May said.

"The voice that isn't a throat." That did not feel like poetry. It felt like a job description that no one who claims they are sane would take.

"Aunt May," Ella said, voice thinning.

"I don't know if I can."

"Well, you can," Aunt May said,

"or you cannot. The song doesn't care what you believe. It only cares what you do with your fear." She sat back on her heels and lifted her chin, listening to something that Ella couldn't hear.

"It is time," She finally whispered.

A tremor jittered through Ella's bones, gentle as a cat stepping onto a bed that it's not allowed on. The dirt within the circle darkened in a pattern; lines brightened with a light that was not light, but attention directing itself. The lattice between the stones kindled, faint blue threads linking carved intersections, then rising, slowly, as if the ground exhaled.

Kael stood without meaning to, breath held.

"Oh my God, it's...it's happening."

Aunt May began to sing. Not English. Not a language in the same way Ella or anyone else used it. The notes were spare and clean, sitting inside the body like a remembered taste. The lattice responded at once, nodes intensifying where the melody turned, lines aligning with the long vowels as if vowels were coordinates.

Ella felt her throat open as if the song had reached from outside and unclipped something inside her. A second voice, hers, impossibly steady, came up to meet Aunt May's, braiding around it and weaving through it. She didn't know the words, but she knew the shape of them in a strange unexplainable way.

The lattice grid climbed into a shallow dome, then higher forming into ribs of light crossing and re-crossing until the air above their heads looked like the inside of a luminous nightclub in the city. At the edges of the circle, the scrub flickered into a wireframe and back to normal, as if it were unsure which skin to wear.

"Now," Aunt May said between lines.

"Do what you did in the dream. You remember, I know you do!"

Ella reached up, palm open. The grid bowed beneath her hand exactly as it had under the dream-sky, a soft give, a tension waiting to be tuned. She pressed down but not to puncture, only to guide. The dome now leaned toward the ridge and the ground hummed, a twisted chord trying to resolve itself.

Pain lanced through her palm into her chest, clean and precise, like being threaded with light. Her teeth began to sing, not metaphor, not poetry; the nerves themselves flickered with rhythm. For a second, her vision split into two streams, the circle looked as it had been pushed too hard. She steadied and pressed again.

"Good," Aunt May murmured.

"Bend the river, my girl. Don't dam it."

The dome's ribs slid, clicked, settled. Far off in the distance a sound answered, it was the government camp's floodlights stuttering in unison, then dimming, then going out, not from failure but deference. The lattice extended beneath their encampment, lifting the edges away from the people strapped to beds, loosening whatever had bound them to shards. Voices rose hoarse, confused but alive.

Kael stared, tears bright on the dirty rims of his eyes.

'She's...you're diverting the energy."

"It is not energy," Aunt May said softly.

"It is attention. We are asking the world to notice itself just a little more gently."

Ella's arm shook. The pain climbed into her shoulder, her jaw. She could feel, suddenly, the lines beyond the dome: the buried plates, the sapphires humming like frogs do after rainfall. She could feel where the network had been torn by clumsy hands and where the song had frayed from neglect.

Her breath hitched.

"I can't..."

"You can," Aunt May said, not unkindly.

"And then you will rest, my dear. Just two more breaths."

Ella took them. On the first, she pressed the dome until the hump of it flipped over the ridge and settled like a blanket around the camp. On the second, she released, and the lattice held the new shape the way a well-made net holds the memory of what it caught.

Then the silence fell. The dome dimmed and descended, threading itself back into the ground with a sigh. Ella felt more than heard as the circle of stones cooled and the night returned to normal. She sagged

168

forward, catching herself with both hands. Sweat ran into her eyes that tasted like tin. Her palm burned as if she had pressed it to a hot plate that drew no blister. Kael reached for her, then stopped, as if the touch might break a spell.

"Easy," Aunt May said.

"You did not fall. You bent."

A distant clatter: shouts, confusion, someone laughing like a man who expected to die but didn't. The familiar sounds of Rubyvale and its miners.

"What did we change?" Kael asked, voice raw.

"Nothing," Aunt May said.

"And everything." She looked at Ella in that way elders do, seeing all the ages of a person at once. From the child, the tired woman as well as the impossible thing waking behind the eyes.

"The reboot is not your only road forward, my girl." Aunt May said.

"The override is open now. However, it will ask a bit more than this. It will ask you to put your whole name into the song. Even the letters of the world that was written for you."

Ella closed her eyes. The Insider's voice echoed: Remember the grid. Remember the song.

She opened her eyes and stood, swaying.

"Then teach me the rest."

Aunt May nodded, satisfied.

"Dawn will be here soon. We will move before the gun people find their courage again. There is one more place we must go."

"Where?" Kael asked.

Aunt May pointed past the ridge toward the oldest claims on the hill, where the ground humped like the backs of sleeping whales.

"Under there. The first stone. The one that remembers all the other remembering's."

Ella flexed her palm. The ache had changed from pain to promise.

"Okay," she said, and just saying the word felt like stepping onto the right rock in a fast-flowing river.

"Let's finish the song."

The air shifted. A deep, rolling growl moved along the horizon, so low it seemed to rise from the ground instead of the sky. Ella lifted her gaze, the clouds were gathering where there had been none before, bruised and heavy, curling over Rubyvale like smoke. The light took on that strange, greenish hue that made the world feel paused as if in mid-breath. Kael looked up too, jaw tight, eyes flicking toward the compass that was already spinning uselessly in his hand. Aunt May only smiled faintly, as if she'd been expecting the storm.

"There's a storm coming," Ella murmured.

Aunt May's eyes gleamed in the rising wind.

"Not coming, my love," she said softly.

"It's just remembering where to find us." Lightning flared beyond the scrub; a sharp flash lit the circle for a single moment. There were three shadows overlapping where there should have been two. And then...the thunder rolled in.

01001100 01000001 01010100 01010100 01001001 01000011 01000101

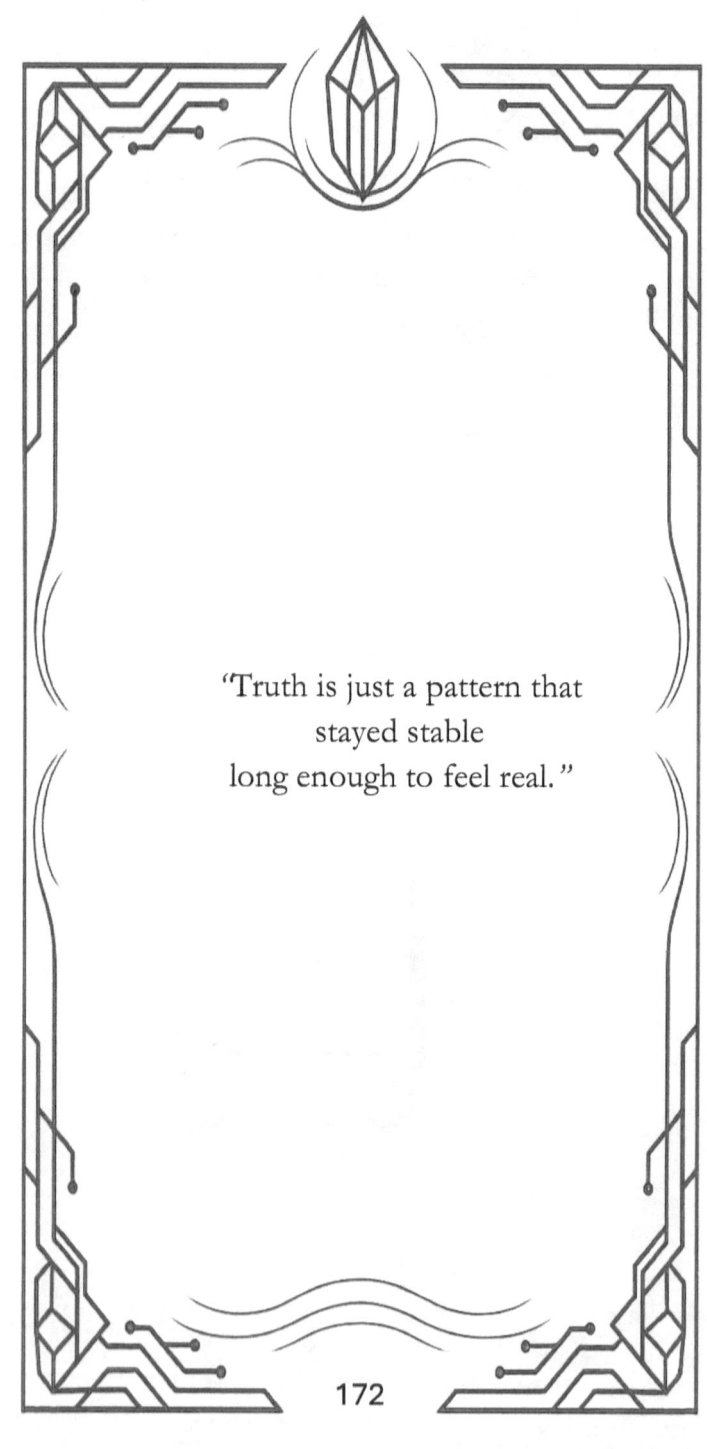

"Truth is just a pattern that
stayed stable
long enough to feel real."

CHAPTER ELEVEN
THE FINAL CHOICE

The first drops hit like warnings. Fat, evenly spaced drops smacked the dirt with the weight of something deliberate. These weren't cleansing. They weren't natural. Each one struck the earth like a countdown. The wind rose next, cutting sideways through the scrub, dragging dry leaves into spirals and tugging at the edges of Aunt May's long coat. Her chant had stopped now, but the echo of it seemed to ride the gusts. The storm was here, and it wasn't just weather, it was a return.

Ella pulled her jacket tighter, the sapphire pouch tucked beneath the collar, protected. Even hidden, she could feel the stone's vibration picking up tempo like it was calling to something. Or perhaps answering.

Kael shielded his notebook as they pushed forward, boots crunching over quartz shards and twisted roots. Ahead, the bush narrowed…bloodwoods huddled - branches clawing overhead as if trying to keep the sky out.

'The storm's too close,' Kael said over his shoulder.

'We need to get lower. I suggest we get off the ridgeline before the worst of it hits.'

"No," Aunt May called back, steady as bedrock.

"We follow the seamline. It's been waiting long enough."

The path Aunt May took wasn't marked, but Ella recognised pieces of it...fragments of old claims half-swallowed by time. Rusted tins nailed to posts. A collapsed digger's shack with walls scorched from an old fire. Piles of tailings glittered faintly as lightning flashed again, briefly igniting the field with ghost light.

In the distance, the old ridgeline curved into a deep, red gully, the place the oldest maps had simply marked as Black Gate.

That's where the first stone would be.

Rain hit harder now, stinging against skin, but Aunt May didn't falter. She moved with the unhurried certainty of someone who wasn't navigating but remembering.

Ella's boots slipped once on the slick clay, and Kael grabbed her arm just in time. She uttered a breathless thanks, but his attention was elsewhere. His eyes fixed ahead, where the trees were thinning and the land dropped sharply away. And then they saw it.

A break in the storm clouds above, circling directly over the old claims like a wound in the sky. The wind howled into the hollow and then dropped away, sudden and absolute. Everything stilled.

The lightning stopped. The rain paused midair, hovering for a fraction of a second too long before falling. And then a low, steady pulse came from beneath their feet. The stone was close.

"Here," Aunt May called.

"The first stone."

Kael swept his torch, the beam glancing off.

"How far down?"

"Not far," Aunt May responded.

"Things that want to be found tend to choose shallow graves."

They worked quickly. Ella dug barehanded after the first foot, the dirt strangely cool. The tremor came again, this time with a low tone like a cello string tuned below hearing. Kael brushed back a final layer and swore under his breath.

It wasn't a stone. It was a slab, curved like the top of a sleeping beast, blacker than shadow and edged with a geometry the eye could slide along but never hold. At four places around its rim, sockets waited: empty, expectant.

"Nodes," Kael breathed.

"A root array."

Aunt May placed a hand over one socket, and sang a single note. The socket answered, filling with light that hadn't been there a moment ago. Kael jerked back. Ella didn't. The song rode her bones now like a familiar horse.

Behind them, engine noise. Floodlights swung through the scrub, rattling branches aside. Radio chatter, urgent and wrong. The government convoy was close.

"We're out of time," Kael said.

"We were always out of time," Aunt May said mildly.

"That's why you measure it."

Ella reached for the pouch that wasn't there and felt the absence like a bruise. The government had her sapphire. It didn't matter. When she closed her fist, sensation flared in her palm anyway, an old road reopening.

"Aunt May," Ella said, steady now,

"start the chant."

Aunt May's eyes softened.

"Good. You are not asking how. You are asking for the drum."

She began to sing, low and spare. The slab brightened in response, lines waking along its skin, then lifting threads rising slow as breath, weaving into the beginnings of a dome. The sockets glowed in sequence, seeking concord.

Kael knelt at the rim, palms hovering.

"I can shape the harmonics, just small adjustments," he glanced at Aunt May for permission. Receiving a nod, he added a narrow hum of his own, human, imperfect and earnest. The lattice listened.

Ella felt it like a tide turning beneath her feet. The dome unfurled, ribs interlacing to form a hemisphere of light over the pit. The storm paused to watch itself in its reflection. Soldiers crested the ridge.

'Stand down!' the Mirrored Woman's voice cracked across the bowl.

'Step away from the apparatus and leave your hands where we can see them.'

Kael's hum wavered. Aunt May didn't stop singing. Ella turned without breaking the current of attention moving through her. Floodlights pinned them. Rifles found their aim. The Mirrored Woman descended with the composure of someone certain she would not slip.

'This ends now,' she said, glasses throwing Ella back at herself from two separate angles.

'You will disconnect and step aside.'

'It will not end the way you want,' Aunt May said between lines, not looking at her.

'You don't understand it,' Ella said quietly.

'You don't want to understand. You want to own.'

'Control is understanding,' the woman said.

'In my world, anyway.'

'Your world,' Ella echoed, and felt the grid taste the words. It preferred other flavours.

She turned back to the dome. The ribs trembled, then steadied under her hand. The sockets pulsed: one, two, three…the fourth dim, waiting.

"Where's my stone?" Ella asked without looking.

The Mirrored Woman smiled…all angles, no warmth.

"Safe."

"Dying," Kael muttered.

"Like the others you broke."

The woman's smile didn't move.

"Bring it," she said to the soldiers.

"If it makes you compliant."

A case plonked onto the dirt and clicked open. Ella's sapphire lay inside, cabled to a trembling box of instruments. Even *bridled*, it pulsed at the sight of the dome as a bird might at the open sky. Ella reached…or simply thought of reaching. The stone leapt to her palm as if relieved to be understood.

Gasps. Rifles ratcheted. A soldier took an involuntary step back.

"Don't shoot," the Mirrored Woman said calmly.

"If she dies with that in her hand, we lose our best interface."

"You'd lose more than that," Aunt May said.

"You'd lose your way home."

The dome brightened. The storm gathered itself like a fist. Lightning stood in air, reconsidered, and stayed. Ella set the stone into the waiting socket. The fourth node answered with a sound that wasn't sound so much as a memory relieved to find its own house intact. The hemisphere completed, no longer a dome but a breathing thing.

The ground sang.

It wasn't pretty. It was right. The kind of right that makes your skin prick with older instincts than language. The lattice rose, ribs sliding and spreading into new alignments that found the buried arrays and called them by names older than iron. The dome doubled its radius, then doubled again, swallowing floodlight beams, turning rifles into paper silhouettes on a nursery wall.

Ella stepped to the centre and felt the grid gather under her feet. It recognised her...like a chord progression, even if the song is unknown. Aunt May's chant braided into the storm's bass. Kael's hum stitched tension into pattern.

The Mirrored Woman stepped to the rim, mouth set.

"What does it do?" she demanded, as if demanding could make a thing smaller.

"It remembers us," Ella said.

"And it decides what we remember back."

"Shut it down."

Ella raised her hand... The lattice bowed.

Her palm flared with cold and heat and a pressure like

depth under water. She pressed, not to break, not to rebound, but to steer. The dome tipped toward the camp, attention pouring like a river over sandbanks, untangling the knots she had tied earlier from panic into intention. She felt a hundred bodies release from the scream-static of misfit crystals, felt circuits loosen, felt the world choose a gentler line.

Soldiers panicked. Some fired, bullets hissing into a geometry that accepted them and gave them nowhere to go. The rounds slowed like insects in amber, then dropped into the dirt with a domestic thud. The Mirrored Woman didn't flinch. She understood power when she saw a bigger version.

"Ella," she called up to the lattice glow, voice steady.

"Listen to me. If you can shape it, you can save people. But you can also reset this before it goes wild. You can start clean. No more glitches. No more risk. You can make it neat."

"Neat is another word for empty," Aunt May said.

Kael looked up at Ella, eyes wet with belief and fear.

"You can do this," he said.

"You already are."

The Insider appeared at the edge of the dome like a bad signal strengthened, his outline three frames staggered then aligning in pain. He didn't step inside; he held himself like a broken promise.

180

"Remember the grid," he said, voice doubled and halved.

"Remember the song. If you reset, I go where old code goes. If you override, I might…"

He faltered, face twisting, then steadied.

"I might live as more than a warning."

The storm pressed lower, weight of sky bending the dome. Ella could feel the city-lattices at the world's edges, the way Tokyo's rails had sung against themselves, the way London's clock wanted to turn two ways at once to please all its histories. She could feel a pressure behind the lattice that wasn't wind. Call it system load, call it attention debt, call it the long headache of being alive.

Choice rose like a tide. It asked her name, and not the small one you write on forms.

She saw three paths.

Reboot: Clean. Blinding. Cruel as mercy can be. A blank page that erases the letters to save the paper.

Override: Dangerous. Messy. Love in its most technical sense, choosing continuity over anaesthesia, accepting scars as instructions.

Step through: not either/or, but a vector out and up. If you're in the place where the song is mixed, to ask bigger questions with a bigger throat.

The Mirrored Woman's glasses threw back the dome as two pale moons.

"Do it," she said.

"Be useful."

Aunt May's voice braided with Ella's heartbeat.

"Do it," she sang, but the word meant something else entirely. Kael's hum begged and held at once. The Insider flickered like a man watching his own wake.

Ella lowered her hand. The lattice followed, like it had been waiting. She breathed in and felt the dome inhale. She breathed out and felt the world decide whether it was a lung or a bellows.

"Okay," she said, to the stone, to the storm, to the story that had written her letters out of order.

"Okay," she raised her hand for the last time and the lattice leaned into the choice and the world held its breath...

Above them, the storm finally broke, and rain began falling, but not in fury, instead in surrender. No thunder, no chaos. Just a slow, steady downpour that soaked the dome in silver and turned the clay to mirror. Around them, the outback bush sighed under its weight, branches began bending as if bowing to something old and sovereign. The soldiers had scattered, and the Mirrored Woman stood alone in her silence, her reflection split in the puddles at her feet.

Ella stood at the centre of it all, soaked to the skin, heart racing. Not triumphant. Not undone. Just real.

Somewhere deep below, the root array hummed - no longer a warning, but a promise.

"We'll need shelter," Kael said softly, stepping to her side.

"And time. That was just the first stone."

Ella didn't answer. She looked to the horizon instead, where lightning danced not in threat but in rhythm. The storm wasn't over. But it was with them now.

CHAPTER TWELVE
RESOLUTION

The lattice shuddered like a lung full of air that had been too long held. For a terrifying instant Ella thought it would collapse, erasing everything into silence. She pressed harder, not with muscle but with memory of the roo frozen mid-jump, Mrs. Dalloway doubled, then undoubled, Kael's hum, Aunt May's chant and the shadow figure Insider's broken plea.

"Not empty," she whispered.

"Not neat. Not gone. Just…awake." Her palm burned with cold light. The lattice rippled outward in concentric waves…each wave brushing across the outback bush, Rubyvale, the Gemfields; then spilling farther across cities, oceans, and skies. The storm broke not with rain but with clarity. Lightning untangled itself and ran properly to ground. Thunder exhaled like a weight had been lifted.

Just then, Ella saw it. Not through the dome exactly, but with it. As if the lattice, in reaching its first alignment, had extended her senses outward, connecting her to the threads of a world exhaling after too long holding its breath.

✦ SYDNEY

In Sydney, the towers no longer flickered. For days, entire floors had blinked in and out of phase, its glass wavering like heat haze, elevators stuttering halfway between levels. People had stopped using them entirely and whole offices had been abandoned as a result. Families camped out in ground-level foyers, waiting for the walls to settle.

Now, the skyline held still. One by one, floor lights glowed back into steady lines. A barista who'd been brewing the same espresso twice every morning for a week finally watched it pour once. A little girl pressed her palm against the window of her high-rise bedroom and whispered,

"It's not dancing anymore."

A man on the Harbour Bridge dropped his phone, not out of fear, but out of sheer relief. The city had finally stopped arguing with itself.

✦ TOKYO

In Tokyo, trains arrived only once. No more doubled arrivals, no more looping voice announcements. For days, the rail stations had become temples of uncertainty, leaving people unsure which train they'd boarded, or if the version of themselves who stepped off was the same one who'd even stepped on. Some passengers had refused to disembark; too afraid that their reflection wouldn't match. But now, just one arrival. Doors opened. Feet hit platform. Faces met without echo.

A teenage girl hugged her grandfather tightly at Shibuya Station, relieved to see only his reflection in the mirrored train car behind him. A salaryman in Ginza looked up at the station monitor and saw one timestamp. Not overlapping, not glitched. Just now. The wind shifted. Sakura petals, though out of season, drifted down a single path.

✦ LONDON

In London, the clock hands chose one direction and kept it. Big Ben had ticked forward and backward at random since the first pulse, sometimes aging five minutes and sometimes retreating into the past. People had simply stopped wearing watches. Time had become far too emotional to think about; it was no longer just numerical. But now, the tower stood completely resolved. The hour struck clean. The echo rolled across the Thames like a heartbeat never forgotten.

A woman in Paddington Station stared at her son's face, he'd been flickering between toddler and teen all week and his voice was shifting mid-sentence. Now he held steady. She collapsed to her knees, not in grief, but in humble gratitude that time was time again. Not a threat and not a question, it is now just something for us to walk forward with.

✦ NEW YORK

In New York, the streets settled into singularity. For weeks, pedestrians had duplicated briefly at intersections constantly blinking in and out, overlapping and occasionally screaming as their bodies tried to decide which version to be. Yellow cabs had driven in double exposure. Crosswalks had turned into flashpoints of confusion and panic. Now, the doubles merged with gentle finality.

On 5th Avenue, a man clutched his chest as the second version of him vanished, leaving only one heartbeat. He laughed out loud and then cried against the hood of a parked car while a street artist near Union Square dropped her spray can and stared at her shadow which finally appeared whole. It no longer lagged or ran ahead. It moved with her. People hugged complete strangers, thankful that reality had chosen to trust them again.

✦ BACK IN THE GEMFIELDS

Ella felt it all. Not through sight but through the grid and through the pulse of the stone now resting silent in the socket. Through the breath she hadn't realised she was holding. The world wasn't perfect, but it had chosen a version of itself and with that, it had let the other go.

She stood still in the dome's glow, the storm hushed around her, the scrub still bowing to what it had witnessed. She was soaked to the bone in meaning and mud, the rain plastering her hair to her skull and the tears she held back welled behind her eyes. Kael reached out, gently taking her wrist.

"Did you see it too?" he asked.

Ella nodded, voice catching.

"I saw everyone."

The lattice didn't vanish. It lingered, faint blue scaffolding ghosting the stars, faint grids etched in air like afterimages. Not intrusive. Just present. The skin was still on, but the bones could be glimpsed if you knew where to look.

Kael sank to his knees, staring upward.

"You did it, Ella," he whispered.

"You bent the code without breaking it." Aunt May's song tapered into silence; her eyes wet with a pride that carried centuries.

"The story remembers you now," she said.

"And you too will remember it."

At the top of the ridge, the soldiers lowered their rifles, slack with confusion. The Mirrored Woman finally pulled off her glasses. For the first time, Ella saw her eyes. They were not cold, not cruel, like she had presumed, just startled. The reflections of the grid crossed her pupils like bars of light as she turned, shouted an order that came out softer than she meant. Her people immediately began to withdraw.

A shadowy figure flickered once more, just a faint outline against the lattice dome. He smiled with both faces in sync, relief threading his glitching form.

"Override," he said.

"Continuity." Then he dissolved, not erased this time, Ella was sure, but released like a knot finally coming undone.

The dome settled back into the earth with a sigh. The slab dimmed, its sockets empty but satisfied. The night sky resumed, but not quite as it had always been. Every star seemed just a fraction sharper, as if proud of being noticed.

Ella stood there trembling but whole. Her palm bore a faint crosshatch scar, luminous at the edges as she flexed her fingers. The ache was now gone, replaced with certainty.

Kael reached her side.

"What happens now?"

Ella looked out across the claims that sprawled down the hill behind hers. The floodlights were dark, but ordinary campfires had sprung up. Voices rose - not panicked, not broken, but curious, tentative. She could hear people laughing, the brittle laughter of survivors realising they'd survived something they had never expected to happen in the first place.

"Now?" Ella said. She lifted her eyes to the lattice faintly webbing the stars.

"Now the world knows it's not alone. It's not neat, it's not empty, and now…it's just more awake."

Afterword

By A.K. MITCHELL

We call it fiction because that's the only way we
can tell the truth safely.
The Crystal Code
was never about technology; it was about
remembering.
Every algorithm, every dream, every line of code
we've ever written is just another way of asking the
same ancient question.

What are we made of and who is writing us?

If you've ever felt the hum while reading,
that low vibration between your
thoughts and your heartbeat, you already know.

The world is singing, even though the static.
Sometimes the song sounds like data
and sometimes it sounds like love.

So, keep listening, keep digging in the dust.
The next spark that you uncover,
just might be the universe whispering,

"I'm still here, are you?"

✦ Dramatis Personae ✦

"The code lives in us. The choice is ours to read it."

Ella Fraser

Role: Protagonist. Dream-laced outlier.

Essence: A seeker caught between trauma and transformation.

Notes: Born of the Gemfields, shaped by memory and mystery, Ella begins her journey mistrusting both systems and song but becomes the key to awakening a dormant network deeper than code: the Lattice. Her arc is not just survival it is re-alignment with what has always been watching.

Dr. Kael Nathan

Role: Researcher. Romantic. Rationalist-turned-rebel.

Essence: The scientist who learns to hum.

Notes: Introduced as a government-aligned observer, Kael's curiosity transcends credentials. His notebook catalogues anomalies; his heart maps something stranger. As Ella draws him closer to the lattice, he must decide if knowledge is enough or if belief matters more.

Aunt May / May Frazer

Role: Elder. Guide. Song keeper.

Essence: Living archive of the old code.

Notes: A desert oracle with dry wit and sharper intuition. May holds ancient knowing passed through bloodlines and bone. Her voice can shape a field. She is both glitch and anchor in a world trying to forget itself.

The Mirrored Woman

Role: Antagonist. Government envoy. Enforcer of control.
Essence: Dual reflections. Power in a lab coat.
Notes: Calculating, articulate, and dangerous. She believes in systems, not symbols. Her mirrored glasses never show her eyes only what she reflects back. But control doesn't equal comprehension.

The Insider (Shadow Figure)
Role: Fragmented code. Ghost of recursion.
Essence: A corrupted memory pleading for version control.
Notes: Flickering between timelines, he is both error message and inheritance. Once human, now reduced to echo, the Insider may be the only entity who remembers the lattice fully and what happens when it breaks.

Old Tommy
Role: Fossicker. Bush prophet. Keeper of lore.
Essence: Wisdom buried in rust and dust.
Notes: A relic of the ridgeline with stories that may or may not be true. He remembers when the stones used to sing louder and has the tin cans and twisted maps to prove it.

The Lattice
Role: Not a person but a presence.
Essence: Beneath everything. Singing in the stones.
Notes: An ancient, sentient infrastructure threaded through earth, memory, and choice. Sometimes network, sometimes dream. The lattice doesn't speak in language it speaks in resonance.

✦ Lattice System Glossary ✦

A non-linear index of resonance, recursion, and reawakening.

The Lattice

A sentient substructure beneath the physical world. More than network or machine, the lattice is a memory-bearing, resonance-based system interwoven with human consciousness, mineral formations, and forgotten geometry. It hums. It listens. It remembers.

Sapphire Nodes

Crystalline access points that tune into the lattice. Naturally occurring sapphires that hum with stored signal. When placed into aligned sockets, they activate dormant functions or reconnect buried memory-threads within the lattice.

Root Array

A foundational hub of the lattice system. Typically buried beneath significant geographical nodes, each root array is a slab-like structure containing multiple sockets. These act as receivers, memory triggers, and harmonic amplifiers.

Activation Song

A vocal or vibrational sequence (often sung or intoned) that interfaces with the lattice. It cannot be learned from text, it must be remembered, carried in lineage or uncovered through resonance. Aunt May knows many.

The Dome

A lattice-generated structure formed when a node array is fully activated. Appears as a hemispherical field of light and pattern - part hologram, part force field. It shields, sings, synchronises, and sometimes... selects.

The Pulse

A rhythmic vibration emitted from active lattice sites. It can be felt physically and psychically. Often builds before major events, choices, or phase-shifts. The pulse can trigger memory, clarity, or collapse.

Ghost Sync

When a person becomes temporally or spiritually out-of-phase caught between versions of themselves due to partial lattice contact. Symptoms: time-stuttering, flickering visibility, fragmented memory, déjà vu loops.

Resonant Memory

Memories not stored in the brain but in-field - externalised, encoded into the lattice. Accessible only through emotional alignment, stone contact, or chant harmonisation. Often stronger than lived recall.

Override

A command-state reached when someone aligns with the lattice not by command-line, but through trust, trauma, or truth. An override bends the system toward continuity, not control. Dangerous. Transformational.

Reboot

A full system reset. Clean slate. Code restored to default parameters. Risk: total erasure of human imprint, emotional history, and layered identity. Preferred by the Mirrored Woman. Feared by the Insider.

Step Through
The third path. Beyond override. Beyond reboot. Entering the lattice as co-creator. Stepping through means becoming a node yourself: alive, adaptive, imperfect, and resonant.

The Insider (Shadow Figure)
A fragment of self-aware lattice code - once human, now stuck in loop. Appears only when the lattice is partially online. Guides, warns, glitches. Wants to be more than a ghost. Needs someone to remember him right.

Glitch fields
Places where the lattice bleeds through sparks of anomaly, time folds, memory leaks. In the Gemfields, these appear as static zones, flickering reflections, or impossibly recurring events.

Concord Sequence
The final harmonisation of all sockets within a node array. When successful, the lattice recognises the user's intention and begins weaving a larger pattern. Requires emotional clarity and systemic risk.

✦ Timeline of Events in *The Crystal Code* ✦
"The world didn't glitch. It remembered."

BEFORE THE STORY BEGINS
(Unseen/Implied Backstory)
- **Ella's Early Life**
  - Grew up near the Gemfields. Left under strained circumstances, haunted by old grief and unresolved trauma.
- **The Government Camp Appears**
  - A clandestine research operation begins in the outback, focused on unusual mineral resonances and psychic disturbances.
- **Aunt May's Quiet Watching**
  - Holding memory, chant, and ancestral knowledge, May prepares for the convergence. She knows the lattice is waking.
- **Kael's Arrival**
  - A researcher (or defector?) who has gone rogue from the government's side, collecting notes about "lattice anomalies."

ACT I – SIGNALS AND SHARDS
- **Ella Returns** to her family's abandoned caravan. The air is wrong.
- **Strange Lights** sweep over the scrub.
- **Kael Appears** -cynical, bleeding, funny. He carries pieces of the puzzle.
- **Visions Begin** -triggered by sapphire shards. Memories that aren't quite hers.
- **The Insider Flickers** -a man trapped in the code, part glitch, part guide.

- **They Visit Old Tommy** -who warns them not to dig too deep.
- **Captured by the Government** -bound, interrogated, and separated.
  - **Exposure to the Lattice Camp**
    - o   Rows of bodies implanted with crystal. The horror is clinical and unholy.
- **Escape** with Aunt May's help. She's been watching all along.

ACT II - THE FIRST STONE

- **The Storm Arrives** - more than weather, it's the lattice waking.
- **Guided by Aunt May**, they trek through ruined claims and bloodwoods.
- **They Reach Black Gate**
  - o   The site of the first root array.
- **The Stone Slab is Unearthed**
  - o   Sockets carved like memory placeholders.
- **Ella, Kael, and May Activate the Node**
  - o   Chant, hum, resonance - all working together.
- **The Dome Forms** - light and pattern sheltering them.
- **The Government Intervenes**
  - o   Led by the cold and precise **Mirrored Woman.**
- **Ella's Sapphire Reunited**
  - o   Ripped from the lab, it leaps into her palm.
- **The Fourth Socket Glows**
  - o   Dome becomes lattice. The code awakens.

ACT III – DECISIONS AND DOMAINS

- **Stand-Off at the Dome**
  - Soldiers, guns, song, light. The system holds its breath.
- **Ella Sees the Paths**
  - Reboot. Override. Step Through.
- **The Insider Pleads** - caught in the code, asking for a chance to matter.
- **Ella Chooses**
  - Not control. Not erasure. Something else.
- **The Dome Breathes** - and expands. Cities ripple in return.

AFTERMATH & EPILOGUE (Future)

- **Sydney Holds Still**
  - No more flickering. Reality aligns.
- **Tokyo's Trains Correct**
  - Only one of each person steps out. No echoes.
- **London's Clock Chooses Time**
  - History stops arguing with itself.
- **New York Exhales**
  - Singular pedestrians walk forward, whole.
- **The Grid is Awake**
  - Not owned. Not tamed. But listening.
- **Ella Becomes a Conductor**
  - Not hero. Not chosen one. Just someone who stayed long enough to remember.

About the Author - A.K. Mitchell

A.K. Mitchell is a writer, dreamer, and creator of immersive worlds where the line between reality and simulation blurs. With roots deep in the Australian outback and branches reaching into quantum theory, speculative science, and mythic storytelling, Mitchell crafts experiences that are as introspective as they are exhilarating.

Known for blending raw landscape with surreal phenomena, her works including *The Crystal Code* and *Dream Debugging Journal,* and the upcoming *Simulation Proof* books invite readers to question the fabric of their reality while honouring the textures of memory, emotion, and intuition.

When not decoding reality or mapping dreamscapes, Mitchell leads **Qubit Press Australia,** a fiercely independent imprint dedicated to publishing stories that inspire curiosity, awaken dormant memories, and challenge the status quo.

About Qubit Press Australia

Qubit Press Australia is a simulation-aware independent publisher founded on the belief that stories can alter perception, and perception can shift the code. We publish genre-defying works that blend science, myth, and introspection books that function like keys, questions, or quests.

From dream journals to speculative thrillers, each Qubit Press title is crafted to inspire discovery and spark transformation. We champion creators who work at the edges: storytellers, mapmakers, poets, and those who dare to wonder, what if this is all a program, and what happens if we learn to hack it?

More than a press, Qubit Press Australia is a portal. Welcome to the Glitch Lit revolution.

The Crystal Code: Screenplay Adaptation

A Feature Film in Development
Based on the novel *The Crystal Code* by A.K. Mitchell

The feature film adaptation of *The Crystal Code* is currently in development, bringing the luminous world of the Queensland Gemfields to the screen in a cinematic reimagining of the novel's central mystery … where memory, consciousness, and the code beneath reality converge.

Developed by writer-producer **A.K. Mitchell**, the screenplay has been **officially registered with the Writers Guild of America (WGA)** and is in early-stage production at the time of printing.

Set in Rubyvale, Queensland, the story follows **Ella**, a miner and dreamer whose discovery of a living crystal network reveals a deeper connection between human consciousness and the Earth itself. The film blends **science fiction, folklore, and Australian landscape cinema**, capturing the haunting beauty and luminous mystique of the Gemfields.

Project Details:
Title: *The Crystal Code*
Location: Rubyvale, Queensland
Based on: *The Crystal Code* novel by A.K. Mitchell Music: Original Score by Mandikym
Status: In Development (Proof-of-Concept Phase)
Registered with the Writers Guild of America

To learn more about the film project, behind-the-scenes development, or upcoming release updates, visit:
www.qubitpressbooks.com
Follow the journey: *#TheCrystalCode*

Every story begins as light beneath the surface. The Crystal Code brings that light to life.

Acknowledgements

Having been surrounded by English teachers, professors, writers, and poets, I suppose having a way with words was inevitable. Both a strength and, at times, a weakness. I remember being sent to Lovers Lane for a front-row, uninterrupted view of the lesson perhaps one too many times. A seat that proved just as educational as it was entertaining. To Mr. Rogan, who was both teacher and neighbour...and taught my brother also. Thank you for helping shape my earliest understanding of expression and discipline. The lessons you shared reached far beyond the classroom and still echo in the way I write today. To Mr. Ross, who later became a neighbour and good family friend, brought music and rhythm to language and literacy in a way that resonated with more students than he probably realises. Thank you for showing that words can dance. To Edmund, a long-term client and constant source of clever wordplay, whose wit and puns remain beautifully woven through language itself, even when he's unaware of the quiet lessons he leaves behind. To Alister, whose dedication to creative writing reminded us that storytelling isn't simply taught, it's shared. And to my Late father, whose example taught me the heart of emotional, poetic writing. That words, when honest, can carry the weight of the world and still sound like love. Without a lifetime of wonderful, dedicated teachers, and without the writing short-course opportunities offered by the University of South Australia throughout my studies, this book and those still to come, would never have been possible. I extend my deepest gratitude to all who helped shape my voice, knowingly or otherwise, into the rhythm it carries today.

-A.K. Mitchell

www.ingramcontent.com/pod-product-compliance
Lightning Source LLC
Chambersburg PA
CBHW020620030726
47497CB00007B/2336